The Voices In My Head: The Beginning
by: Jerry Don Nicholes Sr

ISBN: 9798636058298

Printed in the United States of America

I dedicate this book to my wife and kids, who give me joy and who are the reason I write. Special thanks go out to my son Johnathan, whose mind melded with mine while telling him the story I was thinking about writing. To my family, who inspires me to tell stories. Thanks for listening.

The words written in parentheses and *Italicized* are the voices speaking to Sean.

Today, like any other day, is full of bad news and disappointments. Sometimes I feel trapped with a ton of weight bearing down on my chest, making it impossible to breathe. And then just when I think it can't get any worse, the voices chime in and have me believing that at the moment everything is starting to fall apart once again. So what now? Do I listen to them and believe that they know what's best for me? After all, I've created them in my own mind. I'm the one who woke them up, disturbing the little sanity I had left. Or perhaps I'm reading too much into what is being said in my congested head. Okay, this is the story of a mind running rampant, losing touch with reality, in the hope of discovering the truth behind the voices and what they represent.

So let's take a trip down memory lane. I think the best place to start is at the beginning. So let's start with "Once upon a time." No, that sounds too much like a fairy tale. Let's just start it this way: My childhood was not the best, and oftentimes I spent a lot of it alone with only my thoughts. Now, some may say that's a recipe for disaster; others don't care either way. For me, I had no choice in the matter. I was a loner. My purpose in life had yet to be determined. Let's just say it was forever changed by a line of events leading up to becoming a man.

My mother—bless her soul—was not exactly the soft, affectionate woman you hear about in most stories of family life. Instead she was thick-skinned, not because she wanted to be but because she had to be. Her name was Eleanor, and, yes, whenever she spoke we listened. My dad was the exact opposite: passionate and tenderhearted. His name was William.

These people were the epicenter of my null and void existence. We weren't rich, but we never needed for anything—well, except for a few things that are usually the glue that holds families together, like love and being recognized as a family member.

The family doesn't stop there. I had two brothers, Ronald and Levi, who most of the time thought I was their personal punching bag and whatever else came to mind when they were on their mission of destruction. Oh, and then there were the sisters. Did I mention that I had three evil witches living and breathing the same air in our household? I used to call them Mama's little demons from hell. Their names were Shelly, Candice, and Leann—the bitches of East Fairfield. Our days started like any other dysfunctional family, with Mom and Dad screaming and yelling at each other until it was time to go in their separate directions, like to work. But that meant only for eight hours a day I was being tortured somewhere else, either at school or elsewhere. My private hell wasn't limited to just those places.

Did I mention that I'm writing my memoir from my jail cell? Oh, I guess I didn't. Well, let's just say I'll be coming to that part soon. Trust me, you don't want to miss any of the juicy details. Now where was I? Oh yeah, the beginning of how my life turned into such disarray.

I walked four blocks to school whenever I actually decided to partake in the educational aspect of my life. When I reached Porter Street, which was about halfway between school and my humble home, I met up with Keith, who was my brother Levi's best friend. He chased me for two blocks on my way to school. Fortunately for me, he had a bad leg that was caused by my dear brother while riding in a stolen car that he crashed, of course. And from that they did their first bid in jail, and it seemed to me it only made them worse instead of rehabilitating them. But then again, my family didn't expect these clowns to come out of jail and enter the priesthood. I firmly believe that my brother Levi was born to be wild.

Keith, on the other hand, was a bit more of a follower. He worshipped Levi like he was the second coming of Christ. I'm not really sure if anybody else saw my brother that way. At least I didn't.
Finally, after being chased to school, I arrived exhausted but unscathed, only to delve into the second most hated person this side of Fairfield—Mr. Brickshaw, the smartest man on the planet. At least that's what he thought, and to be honest, I was not sure if he wasn't. All I knew was that he would stare at me, piercing my soul. Seeing him stand in front of that homeroom class was almost like torture. I think I know now what death row inmates feel like when they have to take the death walk. I don't care what I did in his class; it wasn't good enough. But then math wasn't my strong point.
By the way, I never mentioned my name, and I'm sure you've been anxiously waiting to see if I'd screw this up. Well, I haven't. My name is ... no, I think I'll come back to that later. Let me make you sweat a little.
Mr. Brickshaw didn't help much in my childhood development. He oftentimes blatantly insulted me, which later in life he would regret. I

would sit in his class, listening to him ramble on about numbers and equations that I was sure I would never use in life. Well, let me retract that statement. I never thought I would *have* to use. Brickshaw had a couple things that he wasn't proud of—for instance, his obsession with porn magazines that I often found whenever he left his door unlocked while he spent his free time in the bathroom near the teachers' lounge. He always came out with a newspaper wrapped around his porn magazine. It seemed like the only person who could put a smile on his face was Ms. December. Yeah, I had a name for that creep too: Porno Perv. It probably explains why the principal never shook his hand.

And then there were my classmates, the biggest bunch of losers I'd ever come across, with the exception of one—the most beautiful girl God had put on this cruddy place called earth. Her name was Lenora Bingham. My problem was that she didn't even know I existed, and I wasn't about to introduce her to my crummy life and end up being the butt of these idiots' jokes. She deserved better. I kind of felt sorry for her, having to share the same plane of existence with these fools we called classmates. But, man, was she beautiful! I would have given her my heart right out of my chest just to have her smile at me once. Sometimes I would sit in class and stare at her, wondering if she lived a life of luxury the way she deserved or if she even had a life outside these walls. All I knew was that I would never be a part of her circle of friends. Bummer.

And now we come to the big man on campus, the head honcho, the school bully, Reese Gilbert Henna. Reese was the biggest and baddest hunk of disgusting fat meat to ever walk the halls of Fairfield Junior High. I used to call him "Double Up" because he seemed to repeat all his grades, and yet somehow he managed to stay in school. He was two hundred pounds, a massive seventh grader, and towered over the rest of us like a giant. I weighed seventy-five pounds soaking wet, and I had a terrible attitude and no sense of direction. I was that kid who sat in the corner so no one would walk behind me and smack me in the back of my head. Hell, I thought it was standard procedure for a while.

Well, that was until I started hearing the voices—you know, the ones that talked to me when no one else would. (*Make them pay. Make them pay.*) Lucky for me, I was still in control, or at least that's the way it appeared. Fairfield Junior High School was a breeding ground for future criminals, assholes, and derelicts. The only positive part of that experience was the fact that we were all in this shit hole together. And Reese always reminded me and others like me that we were that crap he'd scrape off the bottom of his shoe, which wasn't unusual to us since we spent so much of our time under his foot anyway.

And then I would hear the voices again. They started to yell louder and louder. (*Make them pay! Make them pay!*) I could have chosen to call in my brothers to resolve most of my issues in school, but they were busy making my life miserable. So I spent my time listening to the voices. It's funny how things change. Now I find myself asking questions to those same voices. ("Why me? Why do you choose to talk to me when no one else will?" (*You're special. We need you to help us.*) "Help you do what?"(Eliminate ...)

And then the voices would stop, and calm would come over me.

My brother Ronald was thought to be the smart one in our family, the one most likely to succeed. I always said he was so smart he was stupid. He was always in the books, preaching logic like he was Mr. Spock. For what it's worth, he never talked to me; instead he talked at me. I just dealt with the humiliation. Sometimes I'd even fold inside myself just to be alone with my thoughts, waiting for my new friends, those voices that pulled me in every direction, to reemerge and comfort me. Sometimes I'd have an outburst of almost uncontrollable anger, and I'd go on a rant, calling that idiot brother of mine everything but a child of God. Then I realized those outbursts were only wishful thinking, knowing I was too much of a coward to even disagree with him. Why was I the only Bowers brother who was afraid of his own shadow?

Just as I was deciding on whether I would actually say something to Ronald, like "Go to hell" or some other choice words that I frequently used when I was talking to the voices, in walked dear old Mother, Queen Bitch. Now it was time for her to carry out her motherly duty of starting in on me. To my surprise she said, "HI, Sean." I was in total shock, frozen in time, savoring the moment, because she actually called me by my name. This was such a rare moment that I started to reach for her to touch her to see if she was real or if I was just daydreaming.

Now you've finally learned my name. Ladies and gentlemen, my name is Sean Bowers. And now that we've gotten that out of the way, here's why I'm shocked my mom called me by my name. Usually I was called the little bastard, and my dumb ass would answer to it. But this day of all days she called me Sean. I asked, "What's wrong?" And she replied, "What do you mean what's wrong?" *It's a trick.* "No, it can't be. *Listen to us. We know what's best for you.* "Maybe she just wants to treat me like a real son, something you wouldn't know about." *Don't be a fool. She hates you.* "Why, why, why must you always be so negative?" *It's the truth.* "You don't understand. She called me by my given name, not 'idiot,' not 'asshole,' not 'dipshit,' but 'Sean.'" *We warned you!*)

"Sean, dear, can you help get the groceries out of the car?"

"Sure, Mom."

"What did you just call me?"

"I called you Mom."

"Look, you little bastard, I told you to call me Eleanor. Don't ever call me that again."

"But I thought—"

"What do you mean you thought? In order to do that, you have to have an actual brain. Now get the groceries."

"Yes, Eleanor, right away."

(*We told you it was a trick. Make her pay!* "Don't yell at me. It's enough that she yells at me." *When will you learn that we are the only ones that care about you? We hate her. She is bad.* "Quiet! You're confusing me.")

Well, my relationship with Eleanor had never been good. I think she hated me from the day I was born. She used to say I was a waste of sperm, and that was when she was being kind to me. But, hell, she was the least of my problems. I haven't even gotten to the bitches of East Fairfield yet.

Leann, my oldest sister, had a special place in her heart for me. She believed Mom and Dad's bickering began after I was born, so she considered me the demon child. She would say, "Oh great, the dweeb is home."

I would reply, "Hi, Leann. What's wrong? Your broom broke down again?"

"Keep it up, funny man, and I'll shorten your life expectancy."

"You wish."

"I would!"

"Why are you always so angry, Leann? Sometimes I'd like to be able to sit down and talk to you. Except for the threats on my life or the insults, I feel like I'm just in the way and the world is just floating right by me."

"Look, demon seed, I'm not your shoulder to cry on. That's Mom's job, so beat it."

"I hope you never have kids, Leann."

"What?"

"I mean, you'd probably treat them like crap like you do me."

"Really? For your information, I treat you that way because I ha … Forget it. Beat it, dork. I got enough crap to deal with." As Leann walked away, it seemed I touched something. Maybe she did love me and was afraid to show it, thinking it might make her seem weak. *You know, there's hope for you yet, Leann.* And while making her departure from the room, she did her favorite thing. She gave me the finger. She was so predictable.

Just then Levi walked in. "Sup, Levi?"

"Sup, kid?"

"Um, well, I was thinking maybe we could hang out. You know, spend some brother-to-brother time."

"Oh, man, great idea. We could do things like go to the amusement park together, and maybe afterward we could have an ice cream cone. Fuck off, you little prick. Go hang with your friends."

"What friends would that be, Levi? I mean, I have so many to choose from. Let me see, there's … no, wait, I can hang out with—"

"Stop it, kid. Everybody has at least one friend. Seriously, man, don't you have one friend?"

"Levi, everyone treats me like I'm diseased. It's as if I'm invisible sometimes, and that's just my family."

"Come on, kid, you don't really believe that, do you? Look, I'm hard on you because I want you to be tough like me, okay? I don't mean anything by it. Look, kid, are you okay?"

"Yeah, I'm fine."

"I don't think so. I've been hearing you talk to yourself an awful lot lately. I mentioned it to Dad, and I told him maybe he can take you to see somebody."

"Somebody like who?"

"You know, one of them head shrinks."

"Really, what are you saying, Levi? You think I'm crazy?"

"You know what, you little shit? Suit yourself. I don't care either way. God, you're such a jerk. And to think I was almost nice to you."

(And you thought you were making progress with your brother. "Stop, you don't understand. I think we were connecting for the first time ever. He doesn't like you. He thinks you're a snot-nosed kid, looking for attention. You don't need him. You have us. We will take care of you, Sean. "Are you the devil?" No, we're not. We are you, and you are us. We're your friends. Yes, your friends. "It seems you're the only friends I have.")

"Who are you talking to, Sean? Shelly! Who are you talking to?"

"Uh, no one. I was just singing, Dad!"

"Sean's talking to himself and acting strange again."

"Come on, Shelly, give me a break."

"Why, so Dad won't know you're a loony tune? Too late."

"What's that supposed to mean?"

"It means you're going to see the good doctor again." Laughter ensued. "Hey, Sean, maybe you can get one of your make-believe friends you keep stored in your head to be my prom date." There was more laughter from Shelly. To her, everything was a joke. One day the joke was going to be on her.

(*We can help you.* "I don't need your help." *Oh, but you will in time, my friend. You will in time. Let us help you let us out.* "No!")

Every day I could feel myself slipping more into a dark place, somewhere I didn't want to go. But soon I'd be left with no choice. My dad, for some reason, decided that he could fix whatever he thought was wrong with me by channeling his inner ignorance. Since it was finally the end of the week, school was out, and summer vacation was about to begin, dear old Dad volunteered me to go to work with him today. Yay. Not! Okay, I know my dad meant well, but why would he think I'd want to spend my entire day in a room filled with funky cigar smoke and fat guys who scratched their asses and sniffed their fingers afterward? I was almost at the peak of my tolerance. What would be next for me?

Well, I'll tell you what was next. The strange one, my sister Candice, became the most innovative idiot I'd had the pleasure of knowing. She single-handedly devised a scheme to keep the family focused on her antics. Last year she got a tattoo of a fire-breathing dragon on her back. Everyone else was up in arms over it, but I laughed. It seemed fitting to me. This year she was into piercings. She had so many that she looked weird, and the pink and blue hair didn't make looking at her any easier. But today of all days was her birthday, so I tried at least to look like I cared. "Hi, Candice. Happy birthday."

"Yeah, right, what's so happy about it?"

"You get to enjoy all the great gifts Mom and Dad bought for you, especially the dog collar. A bitch like you deserves that, at least."

"Sean, I'm so going to break your face."

"Come on, sis, it was a joke."

"Ha-ha, and you're still on my shit list today, you little twerp!"

"What's eating you, Candice?"

"You, you little creep."

"Oh my god, do you really hate me that much?"

"Why are you still talking to me, Sean? Better yet, why haven't you been kidnapped or molested by some priest or something? Stop existing in the same space as me. No one wants you around. Don't you get it?"

"Yeah, I'm starting to see It very clearly now. I'm guessing I'm the family curse everybody loves to hate. You wanna know something, Candice?"

"What, Sean?"

"I have feelings too, and one of these days you're gonna push me and I'll push back."

"Yeah, that'll be the day."

(*So you still don't trust us, huh, Sean? When are you going to stop taking this crap from them?* "What do you mean?" *Come on, don't play stupid! You know what you need to do!* "No more yelling. I don't want you to talk anymore!" *Listen.* "No, I won't listen to you. This is my family." *So you still believe in them? Grow up, Sean. A family that lies together dies together.*) The voices were starting to become clearer and more forceful. Pretty soon I didn't think I'd be able to control them. I was so tired and didn't want to fight with them anymore. What could I do to keep my sanity?

The following day my dad took me to see Dr. Pritchard, who believed that he had a pill to help everything. If he only knew how dark my world was becoming. Every day my world seemed to make me feel as if I was being squeezed out of it. So today's session began like this. "Hello, Sean."

"Okay, Doc, are we going to be at this all day?"

"You seem anxious today, Sean. Do you want to share what you're feeling with me today?"

"Not really."

"Hmm, that's not like you, Sean. Usually you look forward to sharing with me."

"I know, but just not today. I've got a lot I'm trying to deal with."

"That's what I'm here for, to help you deal with it and move past it."

"I like when we do the word game, Doc."

"Okay, that's a start. Let's do the word game then. I'll say a word, and you tell me what you're feeling when you hear it. First word: home."

"Empty."

"Empty?"

"Yeah, it's like I'm there, but I'm not there. Understand, Dr. P?"

"Enlighten me."

"It's like this. Whenever I'm home, the family treats me like dirt. I get insulted, degraded, yelled at for no reason, and the list goes on. Believe me, Doc."

Are you in some way responsible for any of the harsh treatment you get at home, Sean?"

"No!"

"Wow, that was a quick response. And that's usually a sign of guilt."

"You know what, this is a waste of time, Dr. Pritchard!"

"Why?"

"Because like everyone else, you're going to take their side against me."

"I think you're reading too much into it, Sean. And I'm not taking their side against you. I'm simply trying to help you find what it is that you need to help you cope, sort of like giving you an outlet. There's something else, isn't there, Sean?"

"Not really."

"Why don't you tell me about the voices?"

A torrent of emotions flooded my mind when Dr. Pritchard asked that question. "What do you mean?"

"Remember, Sean, I'm here to help you cope with your anxieties and any issues you might have."

"Yeah, but what voices?"

"The ones that talk to you when you believe no one's listening."

(*And you were supposed to trust them, and now they want to expose our secret. Push him away!* "No, he can help me. *Push him away! Do you really believe he can solve our problems for us? Well, he can't. He can never take our place.* "Why don't you leave me alone!")

"Sean? Sean?"

"No, leave me alone!"

"Sean, who are you talking to?"

"What?"

"Okay, let's stop for today and pick up on this again Thursday. Why don't you step out for a minute so I can talk with your father? Mr. Bowers, I think it's crucial that we start your son on some medication immediately before he becomes a danger to himself and others."

"Come on, Doc, he can't be that bad. He's just a kid. Kids say and do crazy things all the time."

"This is not some crazy thing kids do. This is a very serious matter for you and your family, and it can become a danger to his siblings, as well."

"Doc, what are you saying?"

"I'm saying your son Sean is losing touch with reality, and if left untreated it could result in a psychotic break."

"Meaning what?"

"Meaning he could hurt someone, even kill."

"Dr. Pritchard, I think you're blowing this way out of proportion. My son is not some serial killer."

"At least not yet, Mr. Bowers."

"Doc, are you saying my kid is like that chick in the movie—what's it called—*Sybil*?"

"No, sir, Sybil had multiple personality disorder. Your son suffers from auditory hallucinations, more like the Son of Sam, and left untreated, it can only get worse."

"That's not at all like my son, Doc."

"Mr. Bowers, I listened to your son communicating with the voices in his head, and believe me when I tell you, sir, those voices were very angry, and they will soon take over his thought process unless we medicate him to suppress them."

"Well, I'm not going to let my son become one of your personal experiments, where you parade him around in front of your scientific community like some freak in a circus. Let's go, son. We'll figure this out on our own instead of taking advice from some quack."

"Mr. Bowers, you're making a mistake. Please let me help you and your family. This patient needs my help."

"This patient has a name. It's Sean, and he's my son."

My dad truly believed his way of doing things worked for our family. It was strange. He never once looked around and marveled at what he created. Instead he avoided it. Maybe that was why he was so out of the loop when it came down to it. Either way, I didn't have to see the shrink anymore, so what did I care?

A few years passed, and now I was prepping for my eighteenth birthday. So much alone time could either make you or break you. I was just trying to survive hell week. Oh yeah, that was when we all got together for someone's birthday party and pretended that we were having a good time just so we didn't disappoint Mom and Dad. Every day was a struggle for me to hold my mind together, especially now that I was older. The voices were now conflicting with each other, arguing amongst themselves in my mind. I felt like I was being tugged and pulled in different directions, fighting to hold onto what little sanity I had left. And then it happened, the one thing I was afraid of. I started to agree with the voices. Suddenly I had an overwhelming need to hurt something, anything. You know, they say serial killers often start by killing and mutilating animals. I was ready to test that theory. I wanted to see and touch the warm blood flowing through the veins of my first victim. Who was it gonna be? The neighbor's cat? Mr. Dolman's French poodle? Something bigger? Someone?

The television was playing loudly in the background. "In the news this morning, police are still not sure why an elderly couple was brutally murdered in their home last night. There have been no leads as to who would commit such a heinous crime …"

"Hmm, interesting news this morning, huh, Eleanor?"

"Sickening is what it is. Son, you be careful while you're out. You never know who's a sadistic killer these days. So what are your plans for today?"

"I'm working on college applications, trying to get some feelers out before I make that decision."

"Well, keep at it. The sooner you're out of the house, the faster I can turn your room into a sewing room, something I've always wanted."

"Well, that's very cold of you, Eleanor. If I remember correctly, Levi's room has been empty for over a year now. What's so special about my room?"

"Well, let me see. Oh yeah, you won't be in it."

(*Just like old times, the bitch is in rare form today. When do we crush her skull and watch her miniscule brain run out on the floor?* "Patience, my friends, we're almost there." *Almost where?* "Now you're asking me questions? What, are you losing control?" *Oh, no, we're just looking forward to playing along.* "There are so many voices now. Where did they all come from?" *We've been here all along, waiting.*)

I finally made my first kill. *Mmm … so exhilarating.* And it was strange the way blood dried so quickly. I never knew it was so thick and red and that there was so much of it in the human body. I thought it was time I started keeping a journal. Then again that may not be the smartest idea I had.

There was a knock at the door. "Hey, Sean, hurry up and open the door, man."

"Keith, what are you doing here? I thought you'd be in your favorite resort this time of year, the Graybar Hotel."

"Not funny, fuck face. Where's your mom and dad?"

"At work, something you're not familiar with. They have actual jobs, asshole."

"Come on, Sean, is everything a fucking joke to you, man?"

"Whoa, dude, slow your roll. What's going on?"

"Okay, well, your brother Levi has been shot."

"What? Where is he?"

"I dropped him off in front of Fairfield General."

"What do you mean you dropped him off? Why aren't you there with him, jerk?"

"Move, you fucking idiot."

"What are you going to do, Sean?"

"I'm going to the hospital to be with my brother."

"Can I wait here? The police may be looking for me."

"What did you do, Keith? What did you do?"

"We robbed the corner store, but I didn't know the owner was going to go for his gun, so I shot him, but before I killed him he got a shot off and it hit Levi, man. I'm so fucking freaked right now, Sean!"

"Wait here, Keith. Just stay in my room and keep quiet."

On my way to the hospital I went by and told my dad what had happened to Levi, and we both rushed to the hospital to be by his side.

"Ma'am, my son was admitted here with a gunshot wound. His name is Levi Bowers."

"Yes, sir, come with me please. The doctor is still in surgery with your son. As soon as we get more info, we will let you know. Please have a seat in the family waiting area."

"Thank you, ma'am." After a while my dad said, "It's been two hours. Why haven't we heard anything?"

"It'll be okay, Dad. This is one of the best hospitals in this area."

"Mr. Bowers?"

"Yes, Doctor, is my son okay?"

"I'm afraid I have bad news. We tried so hard to save his life, but the bullet entered his heart and did extensive damage. We lost him."

"Oh, god, no! Why did this happen?"

"I'm sorry for your loss, sir. Mr. Bowers, there's an officer that needs to talk to you. Whenever there's a shooting, whether the victim lives or dies, the hospital has to report it to the authorities."

"I understand, Doctor. Thank you."

"Sir, I am Detective Benton Maxwell. I'll be heading up the investigation into your son's death."

"So tell me, Detective, what have you found out?"

"I'll get to that in a minute, sir. First, I have to ask you some questions."

"Anything you need, Detective."

"Well, first, do you know the man who dropped your son off to the hospital?"

"No, I was at work when I got the news he had been shot."

"How did you find that out, sir?"

"My son Sean."

"And where can I find Sean?"

"He's right here. Wait a minute, where did he go? Sean!"

"It's okay, sir. He probably went to the bathroom or something."

I was on my way to the house to confront the idiot that got my brother killed. My dad finally got around to calling Eleanor to give her the bad news. She arrived at the hospital a short time later with my sisters. At some point I'd probably be the one to contact my only remaining brother, Ronald, who was away at school. Mom and Dad were probably still talking to the police at the hospital. And suddenly I was overwhelmed with anger, and I knew just where to direct it. I arrived home to find Keith still in my room, waiting and sweating profusely like a heroin junky that just ran out of dope. "Hey, Sean. Tell me, man, is he doing okay?"

(*Wait, before you answer that, Sean, this is an opportunity of a lifetime. Let us handle this for you. We will make him pay dearly for what he's done.*) "Sure, Keith, the doctors say he'll make a full recovery." (*Very good. You're a quick study, my friend. Let's get him away from the house and take him somewhere he thinks he'll be safe.*) "But I don't think you should stay here."

"What do you think, I'm gonna go home, where they can pick me up and take me to jail for murder? I don't think so, Sean."

"No, of course not. I was going to suggest we go to our old haunt when we were kids and let you hide out there. They'll never find you there. Come on, I'll help you."

"Damn, Sean, you're the best, and to think I treated you like crap all these years. Here you are, saving my ass. Thanks, bro."

"Yeah, no problem, Keith. After all, my brother would have wanted me to help you—I mean he told me to come back here and help you. This was all Levi's idea. Let's hurry." We arrived at the secret place where we played as kids. "Hey, Sean, I'll never forget what you're doing for me, man. You got a heart just like your brother, man."

"Yeah, it's cool, Keith. You're his best friend. He would do the same, bro. Just stay here and stay out of sight. I'll bring you some food and something to drink in about an hour. Now I have to go back to the house to call my brother Ronald. See ya later."

I rushed home to call Ronald to let him know what had happened. "Hello, may I speak to Ronald Bowers, please?"

"Sure, hold on. I have to go find him." There was yelling in the background. "Hey, Ron, telephone!"

"Who is it?"

"How the fuck should I know!"

"Hello, this is Ron."

"Hey, bro, it's me, Sean."

"What do you want, asshole?"

"We have an emergency at home."

"Well, what is it?"

"Levi's been shot!"

There was silence on the phone. "Where is he?"

"He's at Fairfield General. Is he—"

"Yeah, we lost him, man."

"Fuck! I'll catch the next flight out."

"Okay, man."

"Hey, Sean, I'm sorry, lil bro, for calling you an asshole."

"Don't worry about it. Just get home as soon as you can."

When I hung up the phone, Eleanor and Dad walked through the door with the bitches of Fairfield in tow. They were all wailing like sea lions off the shores of California. And now Dad began to yell at me just out of the blue. "Where the hell were you, Sean? I was talking to the detective, and we turned around, and you were nowhere to be found! How could you just walk out without saying anything to anyone?"

"Dad, calm down. I came home to contact Ronald before he started classes for the day."

"Were you able to reach him?"

"Yeah, he's taking the next flight out. Sorry, Dad."

"It's okay, son. This is a rough time for all of us."

"Dad, what'll we do now?"

"We start making arrangements for your brother to be put in his final resting place."

"Did the detective have any leads?"

"Well, he was going to check the store's surveillance to see if he can find a suspect or suspects."

Just then Eleanor chimed in, screaming at the top of her lungs, "Why couldn't it have been you? Why did it have to be Levi?"

"Eleanor! Don't say things like that."

"It's okay, Dad. I'm used to being blamed for everything that happens in this family. Hey, Eleanor, maybe now you should reconsider using my room as your sewing room. I mean, it's not like Levi's coming back home."

"You bastard, how could you say something that cold in our time of bereavement?"

"I guess I learned from the best ... Mommy! I'm out of here."

"Sean?"

"It's okay, Candice. I'll be fine. I just need some air."

"Mom, why must you always torture him? It's like you breed hate into our family."

"Candice! Mind your manners. That's your mother you're talking to."

"Dad, stop being weak, and grow some balls. She just put the finishing touches on destroying our family, and you stood by while she did it. I'm going to my room so I don't have to look at her anymore."

"Shelly, can you and Leann fix some food? We need to eat and keep up our strength."

"Seriously, Dad!"

"That's it? Go fix some food? That's your response to fixing this problem? You're just going to ignore the fact that our dear mother, your wife, just told our brother she wished he was dead, and you think if we eat something it'll make everything all right? Screw you! I'm going to check on Candice."

"Leann?"

"Let her go, Dad. I can fix some food. It's okay."

"Thank you, Shelly."

Again I found myself distant from my own family. Leave it to the queen bitch Eleanor to set the tone for a tragic event in our family. But the real tragedy was those self-centered, manipulative assholes I called family. Not to worry though, I had bigger fish to fry.

The door made a creaking noise while being opened. "That you, Sean?"

"Yeah, I brought you some food. Are you hungry yet?"

"Man, I'm starving. Let's eat. So how's Levi holding up?"

"He's doing great. He told me to tell you everything is going to be okay. Just hang in there."

"That's great news, bro. I've been sweating bullets, sitting in this old building. You know what's funny? We played in this building for so many years, and no one was the wiser. We used to climb up those rails and jump off onto a pile of old mattresses that we used to get out of the alley behind the old mattress factory over on Fifteenth. You remember that, Sean?"

"Yeah, I remember. I also remember you and Levi tying a rope around my ankles and hanging me upside down over that ledge until I wet my pants, so I'm sorry if I didn't get the same thrill you did."

"Come on, kid, we didn't mean anything by it.

(*This is our chance. He has his back turned. Pick up the pipe and hit him!* "No, wait!" *No time. Kill him! It's what you want. Do it!*) So I did it. I bludgeoned him to death, and man, did it feel good. The way his warm blood was spraying with every blow up against my body—there was something very angelic about that experience. (*You did well.* "Did I?" *Oh, yes, you hesitated for a minute, but then you came through for us. Next time you will be rewarded with a special treat. Now get cleaned up. We have work to do. This is only the beginning.*) I finally got home, even though I wasn't looking forward to seeing the queen bitch, but I was home all the same.

"Sean? I didn't see you come in."

"Hey, Ronald. I'm glad you made it okay. When did you get home?"

"Over an hour ago. So where you been, Sean?"

"Out. I had to get some air."

"What's that on your face? Is that blood? Oh, man, you reek. What the hell is that smell?"

"What's with all the questions, Ronald? Don't you have an obituary to write or something? I'm going to hit the shower, and I'd like to be alone, so if you don't mind I don't feel like talking much."

"Whatever, little brother, you go do that. Oh yeah, have you seen Keith around?"

"It's not my turn to watch the retard."

Three days had passed since my brother's death, and everybody was on edge. I was not looking forward to seeing my brother in a coffin. My mom and dad were bitter, and it showed. They spent their days screaming at each other, and then they somehow ended up crying on each other's shoulders. My sisters had been stuck in their rooms since it happened, doing everything they could to avoid my mother. Things were sure going to be different around here now that Levi was gone.

We went to the funeral and returned home to receive guests who wanted to pay their respects, eat, reminisce, and tell the same lie over and over again. You know, the one where they say how Levi was such a good boy. It always came from some gray-haired old ladies who smelled like mothballs. *Oh, god, how much longer do I have to endure this mindless behavior?* Maybe after a good night's sleep the world would be back to its old self again.

There was a knock at the door. "Okay, I'm coming. Hold your horses."

"Detective Maxwell, have you found out who killed my son?"

"Yes, sir, we did."

"Has he been arrested?"

"No, sir."

"I don't understand, Detective. Why haven't you put this man in jail?"

"May we come in, sir?"

"Yes, please."

"This is Detective Mims from the robbery division. He's going to explain the situation to you."

"Who's at the door, honey?"

"It's the police, Eleanor. They know who shot Levi. I'm sorry, Detective, you were saying."

"You might want to sit down for this."

"Hello, Detectives, can I get you some coffee?"

"Eleanor, you're interrupting here."

"Well, I'm sorry. He was my son too."

"Mr. and Mrs. Bowers, please! We're here because there's been a break in the case."

"Well, what is it?"

"Your son was shot during the commission of a robbery. He was shot by the store owner. During the robbery, your son and the owner both were shot. They both died."

"Are you saying that's it? That all there is to it is they're both dead? Case closed?"

"No, sir, not at all. Our investigation has revealed that your son wasn't the shooter. There was someone else there with him that fired the fatal shot into the owner. So, sir, did your son have a close friend or associate who may be our person of interest?"

"Yeah, Keith. Were he and Keith close?"

"Yes, they grew up together. They were inseparable. They even did time together."

"And do you know his last name?"

"I do!"

"This is my son Ronald. They all played together as kids."

"His last name is Curtis. His family lives on Murdock Street next to the sub shop."

"So when was the last time you saw Keith?"

"It's been over a year. I've been away at school."

"Oh yeah? My kid brother's attending community college. Where do you go?"

"Dartmouth. It's an Ivy League school."

"Right!"

"Maybe my brother Sean's seen him around. Hey, Sean, get down here. The police want to ask you some questions about Keith."

"What for?"

"Because it's your civic duty, you idiot, and they know who killed our brother, not that you'd care."

Fuck off Ronnie boy!"

"Hey! That's enough, you two. Answer the detectives' questions."

"So what do you want to know, Detective Maxwell?"

"When is the last time you saw your brother Levi's friend Keith Curtis?"

"Sean? Sean!"

"Uh, maybe Friday of last week. Uh, he was talking weird, saying something about leaving the city to go down south. I thought he was just upset about Levi's death. What does this have to do with Keith anyway?"

"The police believe they committed a robbery together that resulted in the death of your brother and a store owner."

"Wow, it sucks to be him."

"Well, thank you, folks, for talking to us. We'll be on our way."

"Detective?"

"Yes, Mrs. Bowers."

"The store owner—did he have any children?"

"Yes, ma'am, two daughters, nine and eleven."

Another week passed. My brother, Ron, decided to take a sabbatical from school to stick around to make sure Mom and Dad were okay. Dad went back to work. Eleanor returned to being the miserable bitch she always was. And my sisters, well, they were a whole other story. I decided on what school I wanted to attend in the fall, and I made sure it was far away from this house full of pathetic family members. But in the meantime, I had plenty to keep me busy until it was time for me to leave Fairfield. God, I wish I knew what it felt like to be normal.

The news was on the TV. "Hey, what are you watching, Shelly?"

"The early-edition news."

"God, I hate the news. It's so depressing."

"Well, Leann, it's better than the news we get in this family."

"Yeah, true that."

"By the way, did you know that they believe Fairfield has a serial killer on the loose? "

"Oh yeah? It's probably our loony tune brother Sean."

Both girls laughed hysterically. "I wouldn't put it past him, Leann. He is the definition of weird little brother. More laughter ensued.

"So what are you two finding so funny this morning?"

"Oh, we're just being silly."

"Well, how about whipping up your big brother up some eggs and bacon?" The room went silent. "What, did I say a bad word or something?"

"No, Ronnie, it's just that it feels weird calling you big brother now that Levi's gone."

"I'm sorry, guys."

"No, it's fine. I'm glad you're stepping into the role of big brother."

"Thanks, Shel. Now can I get those eggs and bacon?"

"My goodness, do you ever think about anything else besides food?"

"Hey, Candice. Hey, guys."

"Did we wake you?"

"Nah, I didn't get much sleep anyway."

"I don't think either of us did."

"Where's the dweeb?"

"Ha, he's probably the only one who gets any sleep around here."

"No, he's gone already. Said he needed an early start this morning."

"Well, that's odd even for him. He doesn't do anything early."

"Leann?"

"Yes, Mom?"

"How's your schedule today?"

"Oh, let me see. I think I'll go have a new tattoo put on my ass that says, "Kiss it.""

"Why must you be so difficult?"

"Look, Eleanor, we're having a family moment here, do you mind?"

"Fine, Shelly, can I—"

"No, Mom, I'm not sacrificing my day for you and whatever stupid idea you have about us spending mother-daughter time together."

"Well, I guess that leaves you, Candice."

"This is so unfair. I'm stuck with evil Lynn all day while you guys get to splurge."

"Yeah, life's a bitch and then you die."

Everyone sighed as they walked away.

Back at the precinct, Detectives Maxwell and Mims were working tirelessly on two unsolved cases that had some similarities. All of the victims were bludgeoned to death, and they both seemed like the perpetrator was in a violent rage. "Hey, Max? Does it seem strange to you that the Bowers kid—what's his name, uh, Sean?—seemed distant and unconcerned about this whole thing?"

"What are you saying?"

"I mean, it's just something about that kid that creeps me out."

"Trust me when I say this, Mims, all teens creep me out, and I have two teens at home that are probably the creepiest."

"Yeah, but this Sean character makes the hair on the back of my neck stand up."

"Maybe you should switch to decaf, Mims. Let's go do some detective work."

"Right behind you!"

It was early, so I decided to walk down to my favorite place to think, the seashore. This was probably the only place in this entire town that was peaceful enough to actually hear your own thoughts. There was something very calming about water crashing up against the rocks. It was the only time I didn't hear the voices. Even though this was going to have to be short-lived, it still did the job. Now I needed to make a plan. As I was walking by the little television repair shop, I saw on one of the TVs Detective Maxwell giving an interview. I stepped inside to hear what they were saying.

"Hey, Bill?"

"Hello, Sean, what can I do for you?"

"Can you turn that up? I want to hear what they're talking about."

"Sure, kid."

"Today we got a call from a concerned citizen stating that there was a foul odor coming from the building next door to the building in which she resided. As we entered the abandoned building, we came upon a body of a young male between the ages of twenty to thirty years. The body was identified as Keith Curtis, who resides on Murdock Street.

"My goodness, I can't believe this is happening right here in our little town of Fairfield, Sean."

"Yeah, shit's crazy, Bill. Well, I'm out."

"Where are you off to, Sean?"

"Oh, uh, I got some business to take care of."

"Well, give my best to William and Eleanor for me."

"Will do, Bill. See ya." *Oh my god, I can't believe they found that piece of shit Keith already. Got to do a better job next time. I'm getting sloppy.* I thought I would head home while it was still early to regroup. I hoped all the family was up and out of the house, because I really didn't feel like hearing the third-degree questioning from them.

"I guess we're going to have to learn to deal with our losses better. I don't think it's healthy to have so much division in our family, Eleanor."

"Are you saying it's my fault we're this way, William?"

"No, of course not, honey. I'm saying we could both be a bit more attentive to their needs."

"Exactly whose needs are you talking about, William?"

"All of our children, Ellie. Come on, stop being sarcastic."

"Are you forgetting we are now one child short, William, and suddenly you're becoming the concerned father?"

"I've always been good to our children, and you're out of line, Eleanor!"

"Okay, you keep telling yourself that, William. Keep sticking your head in the sand and hoping that these problems that you seem to think are just hiccups will go away that easy."

"Why do you do that, Eleanor?"

"What might that be, dear?"

"Turn everything I say around to fit so you don't have to feel guilty."

"Guilty! Why would I feel guilty?"

"The same reason you're standing here yelling, because you can't deal with the reality of you being the—"

"The what, William?"

"Well, the reason our children hate us."

The door slammed.

"No, Dad, we don't hate you, just the queen bitch."

"Sean!"

"No, Dad, it's time the truth come out in the open."

Just then the rest of the family entered the room. "What's all the yelling about?"

"Yeah, tell us, Mommy dearest, why are you so upset?"

"Shut up, Sean!"

"Well maybe I'll tell them and help you out. You see, Eleanor doesn't want to believe that she's the root of all our family's problems. And Dad was trying to point it out to her when she decided to try and intimidate him like always."

"Come on, Sean, stay out of this. Mom and Dad can work out their own problems."

"No, I won't stay out of it!"

"Finally, Dad got the balls to stand up to the queen bitch, and now everyone but me wants to shut him down."

"Sean, why must you always be the wiseass?"

"Well, let me see, *Eleanor*! Maybe because I'm the only one who's not afraid to tell you how much I hate you! Maybe I say what everybody else is thinking!"

"Maybe you need to back off, Sean!"

"No, Ronald, he's right."

"Leann! Of all the people, I would never have thought you'd take his side in this."

"But he's right, and you know it. Wait a minute, I don't need my children telling me if I'm a good person or not. I raised you ungrateful bastards."

"Mom, you don't mean that. You're just letting them get under your skin."

"No, Ronnie, I'm leaving."

"Mom!"

"It's okay, son, let her go. She just needs to blow off some steam."

"Dad, how could you just stand there and do nothing?"

"Maybe what they're saying is true, son, and we've been covering it up for so long that when your brother died, our emotions finally came to a head."

"I can't believe I'm hearing this from you, Dad! I have to hit the shower. I have a job interview."

"Okay, son, good luck."

"So where do we go from here, Dad?"

"I don't know, Candice. I don't know."

"Why can't we talk like normal families?"

"We do, Shelly. We just yell when we do it."

"Anyways, I have to go. I have things to do."

"Bye, Sean."

"Bye, guys."

The door closed behind me. *Damn*, I got a headache. (*Remember what we said, Sean.* "Not you guys again. What now?" *It's time to put in some work.* "What now?" *Let's play We're Going to Find Eleanor and Take Her Down a Notch. There she is, coming out of the pharmacy. Now's your chance.*)

"Hey, Eleanor?"

"What do you want, to grind my gears some more?"

"No, actually I came to apologize."

"You're apologizing to me? Apparently you're not feeling well."

"Come on, Eleanor, give me a break."

"Okay, Sean, humor me."

"Walk with me. I want to show you something."

"Okay, what is it? Sean, where are you taking me?"

"To see what Levi was working on before he died. I think he was going to dedicate it to you. He's been painting it for a while now, and I think he had just finished it before—well, you know—he died. It's right in here, but first I have to blindfold you."

"Why do you have to blindfold me, young man?"

"Because that's what my big brother would have done to surprise you."

"Oh all right, let's do it."

(*This is too easy. You are learning so much from us. Makes us proud.*)

"Right this way, Eleanor. Watch your step."

"Are we finally here?"

"Yes, we are. You ready?"

"Yes, I'm tickled to death."

"Strange choice of words, Eleanor." Then I picked up a large piece of broken concrete and smashed her skull open. The blood-curdling noises she moaned made the experience all the better. Finally, the queen bitch was dead.

"Okay, Dad, enough is enough. Now it's time to go find Mom and bring her home."

"Ronnie, you worry too much. She's probably shopping or venting with her dainty friend Charlotte."

"Well, maybe we can call her to see if she is there."

"All right, son, calm down."

"It's not like her to be out this late without at least one phone call to say where she is."

"Son, your mom was pretty upset with me. I'm sure she's fine." He dialed Charlotte's phone number. "Hello, Charlotte, this is William. I was wondering if my wife was there by chance."

"I'm sorry, William, I haven't seen her at all today. Is everything okay?"

"I'm sure she's fine. She left to blow off some steam earlier today, and we haven't heard from her, and the kids started to get worried. She'll probably turn up soon."

"Well, if you need me, don't hesitate to call, William."

"Thanks, Charlotte."

"Well, well, look what the cat dragged in."

"Whatever!"

"Have you seen Mom, dork?"

"Come on, dude, you know my name, and it's not dork. As a matter of fact, if you call me names again—"

"What?"

"Forget it, Ron, you're a jerk."

"Yeah, okay, if you say so. You never did answer my question, Sean."

"And I never will, asshole. I'll be in my room if anyone cares."

"Hi, Dad."

"Hello, Father."

"What's up, Pops?"

"Where's Eleanor?"

"We don't know. She hasn't come home yet."

"Really, that's not like her at all."

"Yeah, I was just explaining that to our father, Candice."

"Where have you guys been off to?"

"We went shopping for Mom and Dad."

"Uh, why?"

"For their anniversary, stupid. Tomorrow's their twenty-five-year anniversary."

"Oh my, I totally forgot. Okay, I got to run out before it gets late and get them a gift. Tell Dad I'll be back soon."

"Okay, Ronnie, be careful out." The door closed.

"Where's he rushing off to?"

"He forgot to get Mom and Dad a gift."

"Figures!"

Okay, let's see where I can get an anniversary gift this time of night. Oh, great, Coleman's is still open. They should have something there.

The Fairfield scholastic achievement ceremony was just kicking off, with Mr. Brickshaw as the master of ceremonies. For him this was the greatest thing since sliced bread. This was where the local schools picked the smartest kids—or as I always said, the dorkiest and the girls with the biggest tits— to come together to kick dirt in the faces of the less fortunate kids. For Mr. Brickshaw, this was the night for the girls that were struggling the entire year to save face for their wealthy families, and to pay their debt to him for passing them off as elite students. Immediately after it was over, he had a special meeting place for the girl to pay her debt to him for rewarding her with such a prestigious honor. And given what they had to lose, they were more than willing to pay up. The Fairfield Motel was the meeting place for Brickshaw. He always reserved the same room every year for that purpose only. Room 109 in the back of the motel allowed him to make sure his young guest wasn't seen entering the premises.

Damn it, I'm restless again. Guess I'm on the prowl. "I'm leaving, guys. I'll be late getting in, so don't wait up."

"Yeah, like that's going to happen!"

"Blow me, Shelly!"

"Eww, I'd rather eat my own vomit."

As I walked, the night seemed to whisper my name in a weird Friday-the-thirteenth kind of way. *What's this? Oh, I almost forgot it's Brickshaw's date night. Wonder who his victim is tonight.* Here we go. The Fairfield Motel was home to the weirdest weirdoes. *Ha-ha, that's funny even for me. Wait a minute, I'm in luck.* She headed to his room, but Sean couldn't quite make out her face yet. *Oh, well, she's in. What a lucky bastard. He gets to bang the prom queen or the top girl athletes or maybe even best-looking girl in the school, with his carnivorous appetite for young booty. Okay, here we go. She's leaving. Man, was he fast. Talk about a quickie. Maybe we should call him Brickshaw the speed king. Well, I need to see who it is leaving his room. I think I'll just run over and scare the shit out of her.* "Excuse me?" When she turned around, I couldn't believe my eyes. "Lenora?"

"Sean, what are you doing here?"

"I should be asking you the same thing."

"Oh, I was dropping off something to a friend."

"Lenora, you don't have to front. I know."

"You know what, Sean?"

"I know about Brickshaw and his yearly event in this room."

"Brickshaw? Why would I be meeting Brickshaw at a motel? He's disgusting, Sean!"

"It's not me he's after. Besides, he likes the jocks."

"Since when?"

"Since always. You mean you didn't know?"

"No, I thought by him always having the porno magazines locked in his supply room at school that he was."

"He was what, straight? No, Sean, he's, as some would say, a man's man."

"So who has he got in there? Dish the dirt, Lenora."

"No one yet, but he should be arriving any minute. I just heard him on the phone, and the guy was at Coleman's shopping for a gift."

"This is going to be good. Let's get out of sight so they won't see us. Come on, we can sit in my car. I'm parked over there."

"You know, Sean, all through high school I wondered why you never asked me out. In a way I was saving myself for you."

"Me?"

"Yeah, you, silly. I always thought you were the cutest boy."

"I guess I never thought you would ever consider going out with a loser like me."

"Why do you put yourself down that way?"

"I don't know, maybe because everyone else does and I got in the habit of doing it to myself."

"Well, you shouldn't be that way. I think you're cool."

"Me, cool?"

"Yeah, you're smart, you're tall, dark, and handsome. What more does a woman need?"

"Maybe to hang out with someone who's part of the in crowd."

"I would prefer to hang out with you."

Lenora touched my hand and moved toward me. We embraced in a kiss.

"Look, Sean, there he is, Mr. Brickshaw's date. Can you see who it is?"

"Wait, he's moving into the light. What the fuck, it can't be!"

"What's wrong, Sean? Do you know that guy?"

"Oh, yeah, very well. He's my brother, Ronald."

"Now that the cat's out of the bag, what are you going to do?"

"Oh, I can think of a few things, but only one comes to mind right now."

"What's that?"

"Wait here. I'll be right back."

"Sean?"

"It's okay. Give me a minute."

I went to the motel lobby. "Hello, sir, I need a room."

"Well, I'm glad to see you made it back, Sean. You had me worried there for a minute. So what's the big secret?"

"No secret. I got us a room. You didn't think I was going to spend the night in your car, did you?"

"You are so bad."

After a romantic night together, Lenora and I woke up to a beautiful sunset. We were both feeling good about a night of hot sex in a sleazy motel. But we were quickly reminded that Ronald was two doors down, probably lying in the arms of our high school teacher.

"So, Sean, what's going to happen with you and your brother? I'm sorry, I don't mean to pry."

"No, it's okay, Lenora. It's not like you didn't see what happened last night."

"Yeah, I know."

"But in the meantime let's make this our little secret."

"Sure, you can count on me."

"Hey, let's get out of this dump and go home."

We were both laughing when Lenora said, "I had a really great time last night, Sean."

"Yeah, me too, Lenora. Maybe I'll see you tonight."

"I'm sure of it."

We embraced in a kiss. "Bye, beautiful."

"Oh my god, guess what I just saw out the window, Shelly."

"What? Tell me."

"Sean and Lenora Bingham playing sucky face in her car."

"Stop the madness. That's not possible!"

"Yes, it is, Candice. I saw it with my own eyes. Let's go downstairs and get the scoop. Come on."

"You guys are so wrong."

"Whatever, Leann, you want to know just as bad as we do, so let's go."

"Right behind you."

"So, Sean, what's up with you and Lenora Bingham? Are you guys an item?"

"Oh, maybe there's something brewing—at least I'm hoping there is. So where's Dad?"

"He left this morning. He said he was going to find Mom and bring her home."

"Huh, good luck with that."

"What's that supposed to mean?"

"You know what I mean, Shelly. Whenever the queen bitch gets a thorn in her ass, she creates drama."

"No, this is different, Sean. No one's seen or heard from her in over twenty-four hours."

"Wait, you're saying she's really missing?"

"Yes!"

"I'm sorry, guys, I didn't know. So has Dad got the police involved yet?"

"Yeah, he's at the station filing a report as we speak."

The door opened.

"Ronnie, we're glad you're home. Mom's still missing."

"Where's Dad?"

"Dad's already on it. He's at the police station now."

"This is unbelievable. First Levi dies, and then Mom goes missing."

"So where have you been all night anyway?"

"None of your business, Leann. I don't have to report to you every time I go out."

"Whoa, what was that, Ronald Bowers?"

"Look, I'm sorry. I've had a long night. I'm tired. That's all."

I was laughing in the background. "You are hilarious, big brother."

"What's that supposed to mean Sean?"

I began to walk away and then suddenly turned and said, "Oh yeah, how's that cocksucker Brickshaw? Hey, look, you got something on your chin. What is that, mayonnaise?" As I laughed and walked away, I could see the worried look in my brother's eyes. I expected he would want to talk sooner or later, because I knew a secret, and like with all secrets, there was a price to pay for keeping them.

In the meantime, my dad was still groveling over the fact that Eleanor hadn't turned up yet, and everyone was looking upset and distraught over it. I just hated that I had to keep playing along with the charade. But now I thought it was time to go pay the teacher a visit and teach him a lesson. (*This one should make us famous, Sean.* "Yeah, but this time he's finally going to see what he taught me when he thought I wasn't paying attention." *Yes, make him pay. He doesn't deserve to live. Kill him, my friend, kill him!*)

I knew where Mr. Brickshaw lived, because I used to deliver the newspaper to his house when I was a kid. Now it all made sense to me. Whenever I delivered his paper, he invited me in for a soda. And of course, I'd always refuse and keep peddling my bike so I could have all the newspapers delivered before school. And now I realized why he didn't like me very much—because I didn't fall for his antics. I wondered how many lives he destroyed since living in this neighborhood, going undetected for all these years.

Well, I'm here. Maybe he'll invite me in for a soda and I'll finally take him up on his offer. (*Go ahead, knock on his door. I want to see him bleed. Kill him. He doesn't deserve to live! Yes, Sean, he must die. Kill him! Kill him now!*) I rang the doorbell. The door finally opened, and there he was, the most perverted, disgusting human being ever to set foot in Fairfield: Solomon Brickshaw.

"Sean Bowers, what a pleasant surprise."

"Hey, Mr. Brickshaw, how are you doing, sir?"

"I'm doing fine. Come on in. Can I get you something to drink?"

"Sure."

"You like soda?"

"Yes, Mr. Brickshaw."

"Enough with that. Call me Solomon."

"So, Solomon, is that what Ronald calls you, or do you use terms like 'honey' and 'sweetheart'?"

"I don't follow, Sean. What's wrong with you?"

"Now that's funny, asshole, you asking what's wrong with me."

"I'm afraid I'm going to have to ask you to leave."

"You should be afraid, Brickshaw, very afraid!"

Then I took a vase he kept by his front door and broke it over his head, knocking him unconscious. (*Lock the door, Sean, and let's take him to his basement and tie him up. We want to take our time with this one.*) I tied him to the center pole in his basement, put a sock in his mouth, and used duct tape to secure it so no one could hear him scream. I could feel the adrenaline start to pump. My hands started to get clammy, and I started to giggle like some little schoolgirl with one of those puppy love crushes on the cute boy in the class. *Exhilarating.* Just as Brickshaw started to regain consciousness, the blood trickled down his forehead and started to dry, because it was so hot down in his basement. He looked up at me with fear in his eyes, as if he knew what the outcome was going to be. He was groaning from the large bump on his receding hairline, where I hit him.

"Oh, so we're awake! Good! I wouldn't want you to miss this. What? I can't hear you, Brickshaw. You seem to have a long tubular thing shoved down your throat." And then the voices took over. They were singing. (*I know what you are, and I know what you've been doing.*) "Stop squirming, Solomon. You're only going to make it more difficult!" (*Let us handle this, Sean.* "No, he's mine. This is for me to enjoy. He owes me a good grade, something I could never get from him in school.") I snatched off the duct tape and pulled the sock out of his mouth.

"Sean, please, you're sick. Let me help you. There's no one here but us. Who are you talking to?"

"My friends. They help me."

"Help you do what, hurt people?"

"Shut up, Solomon. You don't know me!"

"Just tell me why you're so angry at me. I can get you some help, Sean. Please let me help you."

"Solomon, you're in no position to help anyone. Do you know what this is, Solly ole boy? It's a hammer. The worst part is it's your hammer. This, of course, is a gutter spike. I'm thinking it's about, what, eight, maybe ten inches long?"

"What are you going to do with that?"

"I'm going to nail you, but not the same way you nailed my brother, Ronald."

"I don't know what you mean."

"Really? You're gonna stick with that story? Oh, well, let me refresh your memory. Last night, Fairfield Motel, room 109, my brother pays you a visit that lasted all night, you fucking perv. Is it coming back to you now?" I thrust the hammer into his kneecap. I screamed violently, "Do you fucking understand now!" Then I grabbed his pants and removed them, leaving only flesh exposed. His legs were shaking, one knee shattered from the first blow with the hammer.

"Sean, please no more. I'll do whatever you want. Just don't hurt me anymore."

"So tell me, Solomon, who's pitching and who's catching in your little game of butt Olympics? Whoa! No wonder my brother was so angry when he got home. Look at what you're working with, Solly. I'm thinking he was disappointed. So is that why you chose my brother, because you didn't have enough for the ladies?"

"Is that what you think, Sean, that I pursued your brother? Well, you're wrong. He pursued me."

"You take that back. You had to have molested him or something when he was a kid. That's how it always is."

"Believe what you want. I'm telling you the truth."

"Liar!" I took the spike and drove it into Brickshaw's other kneecap with tremendous force.

Screaming in agony, Brickshaw started to pray aloud. "God, please help me make him stop."

"Oh, look what I found. You seem to be quite the handyman, having all these tools laying around. Wow, a reciprocating saw, and to think the blade is brand-new." It should cut through bone like butter.

"Sean, no, please no more!" Screaming began again as I started cutting off Brickshaw's leg. The pain was so intense he passed out, losing blood at a rapid pace. I splashed him with water to revive him.

"Now, Brickshaw, I didn't want you to miss the grand finale, so stay with me now."

"Just do it, you sick bastard!"

"Now see that's the spirit. At least you can go out like a man." Then I decapitated him with the saw. (*Very good. Creative, to say the least. Now go get cleaned up. We have more work to do. You are becoming a student of the game, my friend, the perfect killer.*)

Back at the police station, Detective Maxwell and his partner were still left with no leads on the murders that had been committed in the small town of Fairfield. "Hey, Max, we just got another call, something about another body."

"Damn it, this guy doesn't let up!"

After arriving to the scene, they came upon the body of a woman again bludgeoned to death by whatever was convenient. This time it looked like a piece of concrete thrown off to the side.

"Well, let's see if she has any identification on her. Yeah, here's her purse, and everything seems to be intact. Money, jewelry all here. I'm guessing it's not a robbery."

"No, it's our boy. I'm sure of it."

"Oh my god!"

"What is it?"

"It's Mrs. Bowers."

"You've got to be shitting me. Wasn't her husband at the station earlier, reporting her missing?"

"How am I going to break the news to that poor guy? He just buried his son two weeks ago."

"Hey, what's this?"

"I don't know. It looks like some kind of school pin or something. Looks like Dartmouth College. Ain't that where her kid goes? Yeah, he wanted to make that very clear to us, remember?"

"Well, he's certainly got our attention now. Let's wrap it up."

Back at the house, Dad finally arrived home, exhausted from looking for our mother all day. "Dad!"

"Hi, cupcake."

"Oh, Dad, sit down. You look tired."

"Yes, I am, sweetheart. I wish your mom would just come home and this would all be over."

"I'll fix you some food."

"Thanks, Shelly, but I'm not very hungry. I think I'll just take a shower and lay down for a while."

"Okay, want me to wake you later?"

"Would you, sweetie? Maybe about five."

"Sure, Dad."

As Dad started to walk upstairs, he stopped and asked Shelly if she had seen Ronnie and Sean.

"Well, let's see. Ron said he was going to find you and help search for Mom, and Sean, as always, just disappeared. Basically I have no idea where they are."

Suddenly Sean raced in the door, ran up to his room, and locked his door.

"Sean! Are you okay?"

"Go away, Shelly."

"What's going on with you? Open up!"

"I said I'm okay."

"Well, it doesn't seem like it."

"Beat it, sis!"

"Did you and Lenora have a fight?"

Oh shit, Lenora, I forgot to call her. "Hey, Shelly, did she call?"

"No, she hasn't called yet. That means you still have time. Call her, stupid! Why do all guys do that? Ugh."

There was a knock at the door. "Detective Maxwell? My dad just went up to take a nap. I'll get him for you."

"Thank you."

"Dad, the police are here."

"I'll be right there."

"Mr. Bowers, do you have somewhere we could have a private conversation?"

"Sure, let's step into the den right over here."

"Sir, do you recognize this item?"

"Yes, of course, it's my son Ronald's school pin. Where did you find it?"

"Sir, we found it next to a body."

"A body? I'm sure he lost it somewhere, and it just happened to be where this person was found."

"Sir, the body we found it by was your wife."

"That can't be. My wife will be returning home soon. I'm sure of it. She just needed to blow off some steam. I expect her back any minute."

"Mr. Bowers, no, she won't be coming back, sir. She's dead."

"Oh, god, no no no no no! Not my Eleanor!"

"Dad, what's wrong!"

"Shelly, it's your mother."

"What? She's okay, right? Mom's okay, right!"

"No, it can't be. There's got to be some kind of mistake."

"Dad, mom's okay, right? Answer me, Dad!" Shelly let out a blood-curdling scream.

I exploded out of my room and ran downstairs to see what was going on. "What the hell is going on? Shelly, you okay?"

"Son, it's your mom. They found her body."

I just turned around, slowly walked back upstairs, and slammed my room door.

"Mr. Bowers, sir, do you feel up to answering a few more questions? It would really help us with anything you have to offer."

"Can't you see my father's distraught? Leave him be!"

"We're sorry, ma'am. We're just trying to find out who did this."

My father got up from his chair and walked into the living room, where our family picture hung over the fireplace. He took it down, squeezing it like he was hugging all of us at that moment.

"Detective Maxwell, what's that in your hand?" asked Shelly.

"It's an item found next to your mother's body."

"May I see it?"

"Yes, of course. Do you recognize it?"

"Yes, it belongs to my brother Ronnie. He never goes anywhere without it. It's his good luck charm. He said when he got accepted to Dartmouth that it was the luckiest day of his life. They gave him that pin when he first visited the campus. He said it was special because the person who gave it to him believed in him and that he was also a graduate of Dartmouth. I think he said his name was Brickshaw or something like that."

"Thank you, Shelly. You've been very helpful. Oh one last thing, where's your brother Ronald?"

"I don't know. He left earlier to help my father look for our mom. I can reach him on his cell if you like."

"Thank you, that would be great."

Shelly called Ronald, and when he answered she told him to come home and that it was a family emergency. "He'll be here shortly, Detective. Would you like a cup of coffee?"

"Yes, that would be nice, Shelly. I can't help but notice how strong you are given all that's happened."

"Yeah, Mom used to say that about me, that I was always the strong one." Shelly started to cry.

"I'm sorry, I didn't mean to—"

"No, it's okay. I guess I'm not as strong as I thought I was."

"No, that's not true. I wish I had half your strength. These are very harsh circumstances, and you're able to hold it together pretty good."

The door opened, and it was Ronald. "Oh god, Ronnie." Shelly embraced him.

"What's going on?"

"They found Mom."

"Thank god is she okay. Where is she? Mom! What are they doing here? Detective Maxwell, Detective Mims, to what do I owe the pleasure?"

"Ronnie, they're the ones that found Mom."

"Why would they send out the homicide detectives to bring Mom home? Mom!"

"Ronnie, Mom's not here."

"Then where is she? Wait, are you telling me my mother's dead? How can that be? No, not Eleanor. Why!"

"Ronald, do you mind coming down and giving us a statement on your whereabouts for the past thirty-six hours?"

"What? Are you saying you think I killed my mother? What are you, fucking kidding me?"

"We just want to ask you some questions."

"Get the fuck out of our house, Detective!"

"Sure, Ronnie, we'll leave, but we just have one question for you."

"What?"

"Where's your good luck pin?"

"How do you even know about my pin? Shelly, what's going on here?"

Just then Dad walked back in. "Officers, I'm afraid I'm going to have to ask you to leave now."

"Yes, Mr. Bowers. Hey, Ronnie, we'll be in touch."

"Fuck off, Maxwell. Didn't you hear my dad? Get out!" Ronald slammed the door behind them.

"I gotta tell you, Mims, that kid has issues, and he's our number one suspect. Let's go see if we can link him to those other murders. We've got to be missing something. I just know it."

"This family is so fucked up. I wouldn't put it past them if they all played a part."

(We still have unfinished business, Sean. Why are we delaying the inevitable? "We shouldn't rush into things. *He's afraid!* "No, that's not it." *Then why must we always wait?* "Because the best laid plans are

always the ones we take our time with, so be patient.")

Back at the police station, Detective Maxwell and Mims were still trying to find a way to get Ronald Bowers down for questioning, but to no avail. The judge denied their request for a warrant for his arrest. "We need more evidence against him, Mims."

"What if we're going at this the wrong way? Can I take a shot at this?"

"Sure, you play lead on this one."

"Then I'll be back."

"Where are you going?"

"To bring in our suspect."

"Good luck with that."

Mims arrived at the Bowers residence and sat outside, hoping to draw attention to himself. And just as he planned, after less than an hour of sitting and staring at their house, the front door opened and out came Ronald. He stormed toward Mims, screaming, "Why won't you leave me alone? I told you I had nothing to do with my mother's death!"

Mims sat in silence, holding onto Ronnie's every word.

"What, don't you have anything to say?"

"Yeah, as a matter of fact, I do."

"Then what?"

"I believe you."

"You come to my house to harass me ... and what did you say?"

"I said I believe you, Ronnie."

"Then why are you here?"

"Because if we can't question you, then we can't eliminate you as a suspect in your mother's death. Look, I'm playing a hunch here, but I believe you're being set up to take the fall for this. Now all I have to do is convince Maxwell."

"Well, let's go to the station and convince him then."

"Mims, I don't see why he wouldn't listen to you."

"I wish it were that easy, kid."

They arrived at the station. Maxwell was sitting at his desk, looking over in disbelief.

"Hey, wait in here, Ronnie. I'll be right back."

"Well, well, Mims, good job. What did you have to do to get him to come in quietly?"

"I listened to him, Max, and I'm telling you, man, this ain't our guy."

"You seem convinced. How do you know he's not pulling the wool over your eyes?"

"This kid's ready to tell us whatever we need to know. So let's just go in and get as much information as we can and see where it leads us."

"All right, you're on point."

After questioning Ronald for four hours, Detective Maxwell was still not convinced that he was innocent, but they didn't have enough to hold him, so they sent him home.

"You know, Mims, I'm not really sure about this one, especially after the motel story."

"What, it's hard for you to believe he's gay? Or maybe you just don't believe who he was there with. You know, he could be telling the truth, and maybe we can find a witness to corroborate his story."

"Well, I say let's go talk to Brickshaw."

"Hey, Max, would you have ever figured that?"

"Figured what?"

"That Brickshaw is a fairy."

"Not in a million years. But right now we need him as a corroborating witness for this kid to see if the timeline matches."

Maxwell and Mims pulled up in front of Solomon Brickshaw's house in the hope of getting what they needed to move forward in their case. As they approached the front door, his next-door neighbor popped his head up from behind the bushes and said he was not answering the door.

"I beg your pardon?"

"He's not answering his door, at least not since that Bowers boy left yesterday."

"What time was that, sir?"

"Oh, about nine thirty, ten o'clock maybe."

"Are you sure it was the Bowers kid?"

"Oh yeah. I was over here working just like I am now."

"Something's not right, Max."

"Excuse me, sir, you said he answered his door yesterday for the Bowers kid?"

"Yep, he went in too, stayed for about an hour, and then left, but he was dressed different."

"How's that?"

"He changed clothes, Officer. Look, guys, I know the Bowers kid. He delivered my paper for two years. He was always a bit on the strange side, if you ask me."

"Thank you, sir."

"Hey, Mims, look at this."

"What?"

"The door's unlocked. Let's go in."

"Hello? Anyone here? Mr. Brickshaw? Solomon Brickshaw, police officers! Oh, man, you recognize that smell?" They both pulled their handkerchiefs and covered the nose and mouth because of the foul smell coming from somewhere in the house.

"Aw, man, I think it's coming from down here. Figures it would have to be the basement."

"After you, Detective Maxwell."

"Oh, know I gave you the lead on this. Remember? So lead on."

"You know what, you really suck right now, Max."

"After you, Mims."

"Oh god, that's bad, man."

"Holy shit!"

Mims ran off to the side to throw up.

"Go upstairs, Mims, and call it in. Jesus Christ, you poor guy. What kind of sick fuck is this kid?"

"Wait, you don't think he did this, do you?"

"Who else did it? You heard the neighbor. He was the last one to see him alive. Face it, the kid yanked our chain. He told us when he was here, he didn't get an answer. One lie after another."

"What, you're thinking lovers' quarrel?"

"I don't know. I'm thinking maybe the kid's a fucking psycho, and you have the hots for his faggot ass."

"Come on, Max, chill out with that shit."

"Look, man, ever since you brought him to the station you've been defending him, trying to convince me that he's not our killer, but yet all the evidence points toward him. We have a witness that puts him in the house! What more do we need?"

"All right, man, let's go pick this piece of shit up before he hurts someone else."

"Where's his head for god's sake?"

"Found it. Aw, man, you're not going to believe this shit."

"Is that his dick in his mouth? Let's get out of here. CSI is here now. We've already secured the crime scene. They can handle it from here."

Sirens blared in the background. "What the hell's all the commotion about, Dad?"

"I don't know, girls. It's probably a police chase or something."

"In Fairfield? Are you kidding? We never have that kind of excitement in this town."

"Sean, I didn't know you were still here. Where's your brother?"

"I'm in the living room, Dad."

"Hey, son, how did it go? Do they know you're innocent?"

"I don't know. I'm still confused as to why they would think I did it anyway."

"It'll be okay. We all know you didn't do this. Just like I told that detective, the only reason your pin was there was that you probably lost it while walking through that area."

"Wait, Dad, what are you talking about?"

"Your pin, the one they found near your mother's body."

"Dad, that's impossible. My pin's upstairs in my room. I haven't taken it out in over a month."

There was a hard knock at the door. "Open up, Mr. Bowers, it's the police."

"Detective, what's going on here?"

"Step aside, sir, we're looking for your son Ronald."

Just then the back door flew open and Ronald ran out of it.

"What's that? Someone ran out the back door."

"Officers, please don't hurt my brother. He didn't do this!" screamed Leann.

"Yeah, well, why did he run?"

A call came in on the police radio. "Hey, Max, uniforms just got him. He's in custody."

"Detective, why are you trying to pin this on my son?"

"Sir, all I can tell you right now is you might want to get your son a good attorney."

"Okay, we'll take him from here, Officers."

"So, Ronnie, looks like your manipulation caught up with you."

"What are you talking about?"

"You lied to us, Ronnie!"

"Fuck off, you fat bastard."

"Yeah, keep it up, kid. That's really helping you out, you know what I mean?"

"Why were you guys chasing me anyway?"

"Come on, Ronnie, you strike out running after we knock on the door. What are we supposed to think? I tell you what I think. I think you're letting us know you're guilty!"

"Oh, shit, you think I was running from you assholes?" Ronnie was laughing hysterically. "I was running because Solomon sent me a text and said to meet him right away. It was important."

"God, kid, you are a sick bastard."

"What are you talking about? Check my cell phone. I haven't erased the message yet."

"Where is it?"

"In my back pocket."

"Hey, Max, check this out. The kid's not lying."

"That's impossible!"

"Why is that impossible, Detective?"

"Because Brickshaw was found dead in his basement over an hour ago."

"What the fuck is going on around here, Mims?"

"I don't know, but whoever is doing this is a twisted motherfucker. We definitely agree on that. Let's get him down to the station—hell, maybe for his safety if not anything else."

Back at the station they retrieved Ronnie's cell phone to see if they could figure out how the text he got came from Brickshaw's phone when they knew he was dead.

"Anything?"

"Nah, whoever did this turned the phone off immediately so we couldn't trace it."

"Is there any way Brickshaw's cell phone carrier can triangulate where the text came from or maybe just a general area?"

"I'll look into it right now."

"Mims, the person who sent that text is our killer."

"Yeah, but how did they know about this family's fucked-up issues?"

"That's what we're going to find out. Let's start with Ronnie. We'll see what he can tell us."

Ronnie sat in the interrogation room, sobbing after finding out Solomon was dead, trying to regain his composure.

Detectives Maxwell and Mims entered the room. "Hey, Ronald, look, man, clearly there's something not fitting with the evidence we have compiled against you. But then again, we have evidence pointing us in the direction of you. What gives, man? Why did you lie to us earlier?"

"I didn't lie. Everything I told you was the truth. I swear."

"No, son, you told us you went to his house and no one was home!"

"How can I make you understand I didn't do this? I'm confused! First you say I killed my mother. Then you say I killed my lover. Then my lover sends me a text after he's dead, so what do you think, I sent myself the text?"

"Yeah, run. That's exactly what I think. Where's the phone?"

"You already have my phone."

"Stop being a wiseass, kid. You know what phone we're talking about."

"Brickshaw's phone? I don't have his phone!"

Detective Mims chimed in. "Look, Ronnie, we're trying to help you, man. Just tell us the truth and this will all be over."

Ronald didn't say another word.

"Who are you?"

"I'm his attorney. I'm here to take my client home."

"You see, that's where you're wrong. Read him his rights again, Mims. We're charging him. Leave it up to the judge."

"Ronald Bowers, you have the right to remain silent. Anything you say can and will be used against you in a court of law. You have the right to an attorney. If you cannot afford an attorney, one will be appointed to you."

"Hi, Ronnie, my name is Bobby Gifford. I will be your attorney. Your father retained me for you. I'm going to see if I can get you out of here, so hang in there. I'm going to need some time with my client, Detective. Do you mind?"

"No problem. Hey, Mims? Where did that kid run out of at his house?"

"Well, it looked like he was in the living room and then ran through the kitchen and out the back door."

"Which means he could have ditched Brickshaw's phone, right?"

"So, you're thinking it's in the house?"

"Of course he wouldn't have had time to ditch it outside. The uniforms were on him as soon as he left the yard."

"Right. We need a search warrant for the house."

Later officers were at the Bowers' house, searching for the cell phone belonging to Solomon Brickshaw.

"Must you leave my house in disarray, Officers? We just had a death in our family. Show some respect."

"Mr. Bowers, if you would just stand back and let us search, we will be out of your house as soon as humanly possible. But right now let us do our jobs."

"Any luck, Maxwell?"

"None. We've dismantled that house and found nothing. What's next? Wait, where's your phone?"

Maxwell dialed Solomon Brickshaw's phone number and yelled for everyone to be quiet. He pressed the call button and heard a faint noise coming from behind a bookcase in the living room. "Bingo! Mr. Mims, I think we have a winner. There it is. Wait, don't touch it with your bare hands. We may have his prints on it. Let's get it to the lab and see what we can come up with."

"Hey, Dad? You don't think Ronnie could have done such a horrible thing, do you?"

"I don't know, Sean, but it's not looking good for him."

"But they have so much evidence, Dad. It just seems like the possibility is there."

"Don't talk that way. But he's right, Candice. I'm starting to believe he did it too."

"Come on, Shelly. We were just talking about him being the big brother of the family now, and he didn't seem disturbed by it or anything."

"Yeah, but you have to admit he's been acting pretty weird since he started college."

"You too, Leann, really?"

"Hey, it is what it is."

"Wait a minute, you guys. We shouldn't put thoughts like that in each other's heads."

"You're right, Dad. We're blowing this way out of proportion. But they did find Brickshaw's phone in our house, hidden behind our bookshelf."

"What's that got to do with anything, Sean?"

"You don't know, do you?"

"Know what?"

"Dad, it's been all over the news about Solomon Brickshaw being brutally murdered in his home."

"Leann, I hadn't heard. I didn't watch the news today. Brickshaw was a mentor to Ronald all through high school. He even helped him get into Dartmouth."

"Dad? Guys? I have to tell you something."

"What is it, Sean?"

"Well—"

"Wait, Sean, Ronnie is gay."

"What? Whoa, slow your roll, sis. Where's that coming from?"

"It's true, Leann. I've always known."

"Candice, what are you saying?"

"Dad, the reason the cops are riding Ronnie so hard is because he and Brickshaw were lovers."

"What the fuck is going on in this goddamned house?"

"Dad! Oh my, where did that come from?"

"Shut up, Leann! Candice, you need to tell me everything."

"Dad, he wanted to tell you and Mom, but he wanted to wait until the time was right."

"How long have you known this, sweetheart?"

"I've always known it. I was the only one he'd talk to about it. He really loved him. That's why I can't believe he'd just kill him. Something bad must have happened to drive him over the edge."

(*This little bitch saved your ass, Sean.* "Shut up!")

"No, Sean, this needs to be said"!

"No, not you."

"What?"

"Nothing. I was just thinking out loud."

"Sean, are you okay?"

"Yeah, Dad, I'm fine."

"Is it happening again?"

"Is what happening again?"

"You know what I mean. The voices—have they returned?"

"Come on, Dad, I'm not a kid anymore. Those days are behind me. I was fine then and I'm fine now!"

"Okay, son, I believe you. What was it you wanted to say earlier?"

"Oh, it wasn't important."

"So, Candice, tell what you know about this identity crisis your brother has."

"Dad, he knows exactly who he is, and now that I told you his secret, it seems to me that you're the one with the crisis!"

"Candice, wait!"

"Let her go, Dad. I'll talk to her." I rushed upstairs to talk to Candice. "Hey, lil sis, can I come in?"

"What do you want?"

"Look, if it makes you feel any better, I knew he was a queer too."

"Really?"

"Hell yeah. Ever since we were kids, when I wanted to play outside and maybe ride my bike, he wanted to play dress-up. Except he wanted to dress up in Mom's clothes." Both of us laughed.

"Sean, being gay was tearing Ronnie up inside, especially after Mom and Dad held him in such high esteem."

"Well, you know Dad is old-school. It's hard for him to understand Ronald's decision to pursue a gay relationship."

"Hey, Sean, do you think he murdered Mom?"

"I don't know. There is the possibility that Mom found out and was threatening to tell Dad, and maybe it sent him into a rage because he was afraid. And you know how much of a bitch Mom could be."

"Yeah, she could be Satan's little helper when she wanted to be."

The following day William went to Bobby Gifford's office to see if he could get him in to have a face-to-face with Ronald. "Mr. Bowers, come in. What can I do for you?"

"Where are we on my son's case?"

"Well, sir, I was working on getting him out on bail, but this morning the judge reviewed the evidence presented to him and denied bail. I was just about to call you when you walked in."

"Can I see him? Can I see my son, Mr. Gifford?"

"Why don't I make a call and see if we can get in to see him right now, sir."

"Thank you."

"We're in luck. If we leave now we can see him before he's transferred."

After arriving to the jail, William saw his son for the first time since he'd been arrested. "Hello, son. How are you doing? Are you eating? You look a little thin. Are you being treated well? We are trying everything in our power to get you out of here, Ronnie. Why won't you talk to me, son?"

Ronnie just looked at William and smiled.

"What's wrong with you, Ronnie?"

Then the guard yelled, "Times up. Prisoner has to be transferred!"

"Ronnie, talk to me, son. Please!"

Ronnie just smiled and walked away with the guard.

"Something's wrong, Mr. Gifford. That's not like my son. He would never not speak to me. I'm his father for god's sake. Maybe he needs a doctor. Can they take him to see a doctor? He looks sick!"

"Calm down, Mr. Bowers. Your son will be fine. He's probably just adjusting. I'm sure he'll come around."

"Bullshit. You can't be sure he'll come around. He's in there, and you're out here now, unless you plan on following him back there and holding his hand to make sure he's okay."

"Don't blow smoke up my ass!"

"Mr. Bowers, I apologize, sir. I meant no disrespect."

William decided after leaving the jail that he needed to stop by and check on his business.

"Hello, Mr. B. You don't look so good, buddy. What's going on with you?"

"I've had a very tiring day, Danny. I'll manage just fine under the circumstances."

"I heard about Eleanor, and I wanted to say I'm sorry for your loss. If there's anything I can do, please don't hesitate to ask."

"Well, I appreciate that, Danny. You're a good man and a good friend."

"How are the kids. Are they handling it okay?"

"About as well as can be expected. Enough about me. Where are we on inventory?"

"We were running short on a few items, but I already placed an order for them. I just need you to sign the check. And I've even prepared payroll."

"You remember my son Ronnie, right?"

"Sure. Great kid. Smartest thing that ever came out of Fairfield."

"He's been arrested."

"Wow, what for?"

"Murder."

"How can that be? Ronnie wouldn't hurt a fly, sir."

"Yeah, I'm trying to keep an open mind and pray that this is all a mistake. By the way, where's Stanley?"

"Haven't seen him since you left, boss. I thought you knew."

"No, he was supposed to be here every day. I called him and let him know I wasn't going to be here for at least ten days. He assured me he would hold things together while I was away."

"Some business partner, huh? Let me try to call him and see what's going on."

"Hey, Danny, thanks again for holding things together in my absence."

"Sure, Mr. B, no problem."

As William dialed the phone in hopes of getting through to Stanley, another call was coming through. William answered it. "Bowers and Murdock, how can I help you?"

"William, is that you?"

"Oh, Stacey, hi. I was just dialing your number."

"It's so good to hear your voice, William. I'm sorry about you losses. It's been all over the news. And I just can't believe this is happening to your family. I'm worried about you and the kids, but I may seem a little selfish asking you this, so please forgive me."

"No, it's fine, Stacey. What's happening?"

"It's Stanley."

"Strange you should say that. I was just calling your house to see where he was."

"You mean you don't know where he is either?"

"No, I have no idea. Today is the first time I've come to the office in over a week."

"Well, that's strange. He kissed me good-bye and left for work, and I haven't seen him since."

"When was this?"

"About a week ago."

"Didn't you think that was odd?"

"No, I didn't. He said you guys were supposed to fly out to look at some equipment for the store and he'd probably be gone for a few days."

"Yeah, but I had to cancel because of all the stuff that's been going on with my family. Let me look into it and see if he just decided to go and handle it on his own. After all, he is my business partner."

"Thank you so much, William."

"So I'll call you when I have something."

Hmm ... still that isn't like Stanley to just take off without even giving me a call to let me know what he was going to do. Let me check the company account and see if he's made any withdrawals in the past week. Well, he's not answering his cell phone either.

"Hey, boss."

"Yeah, Danny?"

"Stanley's cell phone is ringing in his office. It's been doing that for the past week."

"Wait, his cell phone is here?"

"Yes, sir, laying on his desk."

As William proceeded to look into the company finances, he made a discovery. There had been withdrawals dating back over a year from the company's account that were all unauthorized. *God damn, Stanley, what have you been doing?* "Hey, Danny, hold down the fort. I have to head over to the bank."

"Yes, sir, Mr. B."

As William was driving to the bank, he noticed a blue Buick that he was almost certain belonged to Stanley parked at the Fairfield Motel. So William turned in to see if Stanley was in one of the rooms.

"Mr. Bowers? What are you doing at this dump? This is no place for a respectable man like you."

"I'm not here for me, Josh. I'm actually looking for someone."

"Who would that be, sir?"

"Stanley Murdock. Is he checked in here? I see his vehicle parked outside, and I wanted to know what room he's in."

"Okay, well, let's see. Umm, Murdock. Here we go."

"What room is he in?"

"He's not here, Mr. Bowers. He checked out over a week ago."

"Are you sure?"

"Yeah, he sent his key down last Friday night, maybe three o'clock in the morning."

"Then why is his car still parked outside?"

"Don't know, Mr. Bowers, but I remember getting the key. As a matter of fact, your son brought it down to me before he left. Said he was checking out. See, he signed him out right there. R. Bowers. I have to tell you though, Mr. Bowers, that kid of yours was acting a little weird to me."

"What do you mean?"

"I don't know. He just kept looking around, as if he didn't want anyone to see him."

"Okay, Josh. Thanks."

"Well, look what the cat dragged in."

"Detectives?"

"What are you doing here, Mr. Bowers?"

"I don't think that's any of your business, Detectives."

"You know what, you're right. It's not any of my business."

William walked by and proceeded to get in his car.

"Hmm, what do you make of that, Mims?"

"Don't know, but he looked like he'd seen a ghost."

"Yeah, that guy is definitely worried about something."

"What can I do for you, Officers? Would you like a suite for you and your friend?"

"Aren't we the comedian today. Shut up and answer these questions, asshole."

"Anything to help the local PD."

"Yeah, right!"

"Come on, Officers. I've been leading a straight and narrow since I got out."

"Calm down. We're not here for you, stupid. Do you know the Bowers kids?"

"Yeah, I know one or two of them. I used to hang out with Levi a few years back. Why?"

"We're trying to find out if he was here about a week ago."

"Yeah, he was."

"You were awfully quick to answer."

"That's because his old man was just in here looking for someone, and I told him the guy checked out over a week ago. And he asked me why his car was still parked outside, so I said that may be but that guy is not here. I remembered him checking out because he sent the key down by one of his kids. See, the kid even signed him out and turned in his key."

"Was the guy he was looking for named Brickshaw?"

"Nope, Murdock."

"Check this out, Max. R. Bowers."

"Yeah, but why would he be signing out this character and not Brickshaw?"

"Beats me. The kid said he was at the motel with Brickshaw, and that puts him here."

"You think this was maybe a three-way love affair, Maxwell?"

"I don't know, but we're going to find out. That's for sure. I think maybe we need to talk to Mr. Bowers. This seemed to have piqued his interest too."

Meanwhile, at the bank, William was talking to the manager about his account. "Mr. Bowers, how are you today, sir?"

"Not good at all, Katie. I'm having some problems with my business account."

"Well, let's take a look and see if we can get a handle on it. Okay, Mr. Bowers, I have your account pulled up. What are your concerns?"

"I think my business partner has been withdrawing money without authorization."

"Well, sir, you are both on the account, so it's not unusual for either of you to withdraw money."

"Can you pull up all his withdrawals for the past year and total them up for me, Katie?"

"Not a problem, sir. Okay, here's the total: $112,000."

"Are you kidding me?"

"No, sir, the numbers are right here. I'll print them out for you."

"Thank you, Katie."

"Here we go, Mr. Bowers, everything you need, sir."

William left the bank and headed over to Stanley's house to talk to Stacey. He rang the doorbell, and Stacey answered the door. She embraced William in a hug. "Hi, William, it's so good to see you again. I've been so distraught over hearing all the news reports about your family. First Levi, then Eleanor, and now Ronald being arrested. This must be a very stressful time for you."

"It certainly is. It's very hard on us all."

"Let me get you some coffee."

"That would be the best thing that could happen today."

"So what did you find out? Is he out buying equipment like we thought?"

"It's complicated."

"Really? Why is that?"

"Take a look at this."

"What is it?"

"It's the bank statement for the store, showing all of Stanley's withdrawals for the past year."

"Oh my god, I don't understand. What are you saying? You didn't know he was taking this money out of the account?"

I don't want to read too much into it. I think before I make that call, we need to find him and hear his side."

"I agree. I'm sure he'll have an explanation for withdrawing this much money from the business account."

"Stacey, his cell phone was left at the office, and that could be the reason he hasn't called."

"No, William, that's not like him. He takes that phone to the bathroom with him to play games while he sits on the toilet. I know he's not just going to leave it behind. I think I should call the police."

"Maybe you should. No one's seen him for over a week."

"Stacey, one more question. Do you think Stanley was having an affair?"

"How could you say that? You know Stanley as well as I do. He's your childhood friend for god's sake!"

"Look, I'm sorry. I'm just trying to look at all the possibilities."

"There's something you're not telling me, William Bowers. Come clean."

"All right, his car is parked at the Fairfield Motel, and according to the motel staff, it's been there for over a week."

"Oh, what does this all mean?"

"I don't know, but I think it's time to call the police in on this."

Back at the police station, Detectives Mims and Maxwell thought it was time to get a few more answers from Ronald, so they headed down to the jail, only to find an ambulance parked outside the jail. The EMTs were rushing out with a gurney, which had Ronald Bowers on it. "What happened here?" they asked.

"Attempted suicide!"

"Damn, is he alive?"

"Just barely, but we've stabilized him. We're taking him to Fairfield General now. Gotta go, guys."

"Son of a bitch!"

"Calm down, Maxwell."

"No, fuck you, Mims. I'd like to have one day, just one day, where nothing gets fucked up. One fucking day. Is that too much to ask, Mims? Let's get over there and see if he makes it. Damn!"

Back at the Bowers house, Sean was preparing to leave to take care of some things that his dad asked him to do earlier. (*Sean, when do we get to play with our fat friend*? "We're headed there now. The only thing I hate worse than a fag is a thief, especially one who steals my father's hard-earned money.") Sean arrived at an old abandoned gas station next door to the Fairfield Motel. He slipped through the fence around the old building and went inside. There he came upon Stanley, tied up from head to toe and gagged so no one could hear him. Beside him sat a briefcase filled with one-hundred-dollar bills, stack upon stack of them.

"I bet you're hungry, Stan, huh? Probably weak and thirsty too. Oh, I'm sorry. I didn't forget to come back. There's just been so much going on, I haven't had time. But we're here now to feed you and give you something to drink. I'll take the duct tape from around your mouth if you promise to keep quiet.

You see, I hate yelling. Do you understand me, Stanley? A simple nod will do. Good, now let's eat." (*Why are you going to feed this fat piece of shit?* "Hey,! I just told him not to yell, and now you are screaming at me. What the fuck? Shut up, I got this! *Who's yelling now?*)

"Sean, listen to me."

"Stanley, I didn't give you permission to talk. Now shut the fuck up!" (*He doesn't respect you, Sean. He thinks you're soft.*) "Oh, really, is that what you think, Stan? You think I'm soft? You think I can't cut it?" (*Kill him, Sean, and be done with him!* "There you go again, being impatient. Learn to enjoy the moment." *Look forward to you gutting this filthy pig for what he's done to our family.* "Wait, you just said 'our family.' Don't you mean my family?" *Whatever you say, Sean. Whatever you say.*)

"Sean, please hear me out. I can make this right."

"How? Were you going to see my father and confess to him that you've been a naughty boy, stealing from the company? You know, there's a name for that, Stanley. I'm no college graduate like yourself, but I think they call it embezzlement! What the fuck were you thinking? My dad trusted you. How could you do this to him? He has enough shit going on in his life, having to deal with my faggot brother. I'm trying to alleviate that problem for him now. Then there was the queen bitch, who nagged the shit out of all of us. Oh, yeah, she got what she deserved, Stanley. I smashed her fucking head in! And the elderly couple over on Tolbert Street—those fucking nosy bastards, always staring out of their windows, asking me who I was talking to, as if they were blind. Don't you see I have to take care of all our family problems? Not Levi, not Ronald, or even my stupid-ass sisters, but me, the one no one sees or hears coming."

"Sean, I don't doubt that. As a matter of fact, I used to tell your father all the time about how smart you are. I'd tell him, 'William, I think you're wasting your time with those other two boys. Here's the smart one standing right here in front of you.'"

"Hey, I remember you saying that. You just bought yourself some more time."

"Listen, Sean, I used to listen to you talk to whoever it was you were talking to and wonder why no one else paid any attention. I'd mention it to your father from time to time, and he'd swear to me you would grow out of it."

(*Why are we listening to him? Kill him!* "No, I want to hear this.") "Are you saying that my father always knew about the voices?"

"Of course he did, ever since you were just a little kid. But—"

"But what, Stanley?"

"He didn't want to believe that the voices that tormented him most of his life were now tormenting his son! That's why I did what I did, kid, so I could take my wife and get out of this hell-forsaken town before it started again."

"Before what started?"

"The killings. Those unsolved murders that occurred over thirty years ago. That was your father's doing."

"Liar!"

"I'm not lying, Sean. It's true. Your father was the infamous Fairfield stalker."

"Wait, hold on. You knew this? You knew my father was a murderer, and you said nothing all these years?"

"I'm not proud of it, but he's my friend. I tried to help him back then by telling your grandfather, and he took William away, sent him to boarding school— at least that's what he told us, his friends. But the rumors started to spread, and people started to talk about him being in some insane asylum upstate. Before he was sent away, I followed him one night when he did his last murder. It was a police officer by the name of Maxwell. He and his kids were sitting in the living room of their house, watching television, when William went in the yard behind the house and kicked the trash cans over. Then he hid behind the bushes, lying in wait for Maxwell to come outside. Finally he came out and started picking up the trash spilled over on the ground. And then William made his move. He rose up while Officer Maxwell's back was turned and thrust a long metal rod that was sharpened to a point on one end in his back. Maxwell fell forward on the ground, and your father stabbed him over and over again with it until Officer Maxwell was dead. After that your grandfather sent him away. The murders stopped, and no one was the wiser. All the cases went cold from that point on until they called off the investigation. You see, Sean, that's why your father is so protective of you. You hear them, don't you? The voices? They talk to you, telling you to do terrible things. Sean, your father murdered eleven people, and look at him now. He fought. He fought the voices until he regained control. You don't have to do this."

(*Don't let him deceive you. He believes your weak lies. He's telling you lies. We never helped your father. He was weak. He let them take us away.* "Wait, you said you didn't help my father? If you didn't help him, how could you know he was weak? And what do you mean take you away?" *He's corrupted you, Sean. Kill him before he does any more damage!*)

"What aren't you telling me?"

"Don't listen to them, Sean. Fight them the way your father did!"

(*Shut him up, Sean!* "No!") "Stanley, I'm leaving, and you better pray that you're telling me the truth, or so help me god you will pay if it's a lie." I put the tape back on Stanley's mouth and left. *This can't be happening.* (*Why did you let him live? He knows our secret!* "Liars! All of you are liars. You betrayed me!" *Why would we do that to you, Sean? You are the one who set us free!* "I'm in control. I'm in control." *No, you're not, you fucking pussy! You've never been in control. We are, you helpless piece of shit! You're going to do exactly what we tell you, or we're going to destroy the rest of your fucked-up family!*)

William arrived home after visiting Stacey, leaving her to make a police report of her husband, Stanley, being missing for more than a week. "Oh, man, am I tired."

"Hi, Pops."

"Hello, girls. Where's Sean?"

"Don't know. We haven't seen him all day."

"So what have you guys been up to?"

"We were looking at some old pictures of you and Mom and decided that at her funeral we would make a special dedication to you. It's not much, but today would have been your twenty-fifth wedding anniversary. So we pitched in to try and make it special for you under the circumstances."

"Dear god, I've been so busy I didn't even think about it."

Just then the phone rang. "Leann, will you get that please?"

"Yeah, Dad."

"Yes, this is Dr. Sandburg from Fairfield General. I would like to speak to William Bowers, please."

"Dad, it's some doctor from Fairfield General. He wants to talk to you."

"This is William Bowers speaking. What can I do for you, Doctor?"

"Sir, we have your son here. Which one? Sean?"

"No, sir, Ronald Bowers."

"What happened to him?"

"It's an apparent suicide attempt, Mr. Bowers."

"But he's alive though, right?"

"Yes, sir, he's holding steady for now, but I think you should get down here with your family right away. It's not looking good." Do everything you can for him, Dr. ...?"

"Sandburg, sir. Drew Sandburg."

"We're on our way, Dr. Sandburg. We should be there in about fifteen minutes."

William and his daughters left for the hospital. Sean arrived home ten minutes later to an empty house. He was visibly upset. He ran upstairs to his parents' room. For the first time ever, he entered the most sacred place in the house. It was the only room in the house where none of the kids was allowed. It was as though William and Eleanor lived in a totally different world from us. Dysfunctional wasn't the half of it. This place was a chamber of horror. All the walls were covered with strange paintings and a weird collection of talismans. It was like they were afraid of something getting in while they slept and maybe wreaking havoc on them or maybe just on him. *Could what Stanley said be true? And if it is, what do I do now? Do I confront my father about his secret or try to find out more? But how? I should be able to search for the information I need at the library.*

Back at the hospital, William and the girls arrived to be with Ronald, when Dr. Sandburg approached them to give them an update on his condition. They looked over by his room, and standing in the doorway they saw Detectives Maxwell and Mims staring at Ronald in disbelief. Leann ran toward them, screaming profanities, and started to punch Detective Maxwell wildly. "You bastard! You did this! You let this happen to my brother!"

"Leann, stop it. Calm down, sweetheart."

"Oh, Daddy, make them leave. He shouldn't be here. He's caused enough damage."

"Mr. Bowers, I'm sorry. I just got the news a half hour ago myself."

"You son of a bitch, you're the same way your father was, always going about things the wrong way, never caring about the repercussions of his actions. That's what got him killed, you know. Now, Maxwell, I'm only going to say this once, and you hear me good. Leave my son be, or there will be hell to pay!"

"Is that a threat, Mr. Bowers?"

"Heed my warning, Maxwell!"

And then William and the girls rushed to Ronald's side. "Doctor, why is he unconscious?"

"We are keeping him sedated. You have to understand, your son wants to die, and after we stabilized him we thought it was best to keep him sedated so he wouldn't cause any more damage to himself. But I'm afraid he's lost his will to live, so I believe if his family is around him, helping him through this, we can up his chance for survival."

Candice asked, "Can we revive him, Dr. Sandburg?"

"Yes, we can. I can inject into his IV some medicine to counteract what we have him sedated with. He should wake up almost immediately. If your father gives us permission, we can get started right away. I have to warn you we don't know how long he was hanging before the guards found him, but his CAT scan showed no permanent brain damage. But don't expect him to be himself right away. It may take a couple of hours and sometimes days, so we're going to have to take it slow."

"I understand, Doctor. Let's do it."

I walked into the library and up to the front desk and asked the librarian how I could access information about the town's history from maybe thirty years back.

"Well, young man, is there anything you're looking for in particular?"

"Yes, ma'am, some unsolved murders."

"Oh, you want to know about the Fairfield stalker. Writing a paper, huh?"

"Yes, exactly, I'm writing a paper."

"Well, here it is. Right here, son, all you need to know about that horrendous time in Fairfield. I can remember it like it was yesterday, and it's so strange that the killer's back now. I thought we would never see the likes of that one again. But here we are, history repeating itself. Take your time. We don't close for another two hours."

"Thank you very much, ma'am." *My goodness, there's so much here, and to think that they never solved one case. Stanley was right. It says here there was a young man who saw someone by the name of William Bowers running away from one of the murder scenes. The news reporters flooded his house with calls and tried to get interviews from him, when his father stepped in and told them they put his son in danger. So he secretly sent him away in the cover of darkness. Wow, those poor idiots didn't even know they were taking the killer away from Fairfield.*

"How are we doing over here, young man? Can I help you with anything?"

"As a matter of fact, you can. You said you remember when this all happened. Did you know my father then?"

"Who might that be, son?"

"William Bowers."

"Oh, yes, did I. Well, let's just say I had the biggest crush on him. So tall and so handsome. It's a shame how your grandfather treated him."

"How's that, ma'am?"

"I'm assuming you never got to meet him?"

"No, ma'am, he died when I was two."

"Well, he certainly won't be missed by your father. That man scared me to death. He always had a look on his face like he was mad at the world. But your father, he'd put up with it, and I can see how it was tearing him apart. Never got to go out and hang with his friends. Always working around the house. He used to sneak out and walk sometimes all night. A few times he would come by and pay me a visit, and we would sit on the porch at my house and talk for hours. It's like he never wanted to go home. I suppose he loved him though, because after he died he was never the same. He became a recluse, and then one day he just left, stayed away from Fairfield about five years. Didn't see him much after that. But when he returned he had a blushing young bride named Eleanor— your mother, of course—and I think she was right for him. And, well, the rest is history. Oh, look at the time. I'm standing here rambling on about you father like he was my lost love."

"It's fine, ma'am. I enjoyed the story. After hearing it, I wish my dad would have married you instead of Eleanor. You seem to have really had a sweet spot for him."

"Hmm, I still do, young man."

As she walked away giggling, I remembered I forgot to turn my cell phone back on. *Wow, everybody and their mother have been trying to call me.*

At the hospital, Dad was still trying to reach me. He asked Shelly to try my cell again.

"Hello?"

"Finally you answer your phone. Where are you, Sean? We've been trying to reach you for hours."

"Sorry, sis, phone was in my back pocket. I must have turned it off by accident. What's up?"

"We're at the hospital with Ronnie. He tried to kill himself."

"I'm on my way. I'm at the library."

"You've been across the street this whole time? He's across the street, Dad. He's coming now."

Ronnie opened his eyes and stared at us, as if we were strangers.

"It's okay, son, we're here now."

Struggling to talk, Ronnie said, "Where's Mom? Is she here?"

"Dr. Sandburg?"

"He may just have some short-term memory loss. It shouldn't last. Give it some time, and take it slow."

"Sean, you made it."

"Why is he here? I thought that he was being watched while he was locked up. Who the fuck is responsible for this? It's you … you sorry piece of shit. Detective, you damn near let my brother die. Well, I don't scare so easy, and you're going to answer for this."

"Okay, Sean, let it go. Let's focus on our brother. Come on, he's awake now. We should talk to him."

"Yeah, you're right, Candice. Let's go see him."

"Hey, Maxwell, come on, man. Don't let them get to you. They have reason to be upset."

"It's not that, Mims. It's something their father said to me about my father. He said I was just like him, never giving up on a case."

"So what, you're a good detective."

"But it's more in the way he said it than anything. It's like he knows something about my father's death."

"Come on, man, are you serious? That was, what, thirty years ago?"

"You don't understand. My father was close to solving the Fairfield stalker murder cases when he was killed by the stalker himself, right in our backyard."

"Wow, I didn't know that, man. I'm sorry."

"Don't be. It's the reason I became a cop in the first place, following in Dad's footsteps. He was a good cop, sharp. That old man had no right to talk about him in that way."

"So what, the guy's a loser, just like his kid. What can we do, huh? Let's go back and solve these new murders and maybe make your old man proud."

"You know what, Mims? I'm starting to like you more and more each day."

"Well, just so you know, I still think you're a pain in the ass."

In Ronnie's room everyone was trying to lift his spirits. "Dad, I didn't do this. What they said about me—you know, the killings and all—I would never hurt Mom or Solomon."

"Is it true, son, about you and Brickshaw? Were you together?"

"Just ask the question, Dad. Stop beating around the bush. Please, I've had a really bad day."

"Okay, are you gay?"

"I wanted to tell you for so long, but it never seemed liked the right time. You and Mom were so proud of me. I guess I didn't tell you because I didn't want to disappoint you. I didn't want you guys to love me any less."

"Come on, Ronnie, you're our brother. We're here for you. We support you in your decisions and your sexual preferences."

"Right, Sean, come on. I know you want to say something smart."

"Okay, Shelly, I see you're going to put me on the spot in front of everyone."

"Well, Ronnie, I didn't lose a brother, but I gained a sister."

"Did he just go there?"

"No, he didn't."

"Hey, lighten up. I'm kidding. Look, bro, I love you, man, even though you tortured me my whole life. You're still my big brother."

"Thanks, Sean, I love you too, big brother. You're not the little brother anymore. When I go to jail you're going to have to take care of the family."

"Come on, man, don't talk that way. You're going to come home with us when you're all better, and we're going to be a family again. Listen, guys, I have to leave and take care of something. You going to be okay, Ronnie?"

"Sure, man, thanks for stopping by."

"No problem. Dad, I'll be home late, so don't wait up."

"Wait, Sean, I'll walk you out."

"Okay."

"Son, I wanted to talk to you in private."

"Can it wait until morning? I really have to go."

"Okay, be careful. There's a madman on the loose."

"Yeah, don't I know it." I walked away.

William watched me walk away, hoping I did the right thing and made sure Ronnie came out of this unscathed. ("We have work to do." *We? What do you mean "we"? You are mistaken, Sean. We are in charge now. You do what we say when we say.* "You don't have control over shit. You're mistaking me for my father!" *Do not anger us. We won't stand for it.* "You are the reason this whole situation is fucked up. Now leave me alone!" *Wait a minute, do I detect your balls growing? Sean, you underestimate us. We are one. We will always be one with you.* "That's all well and good, but now you listen to me. I make the fucking rules now. I'm in control, so back off.")

As I approached Porter Street, I heard a horn blowing. And to my surprise it was Lenora. "Hi, beautiful. I was just heading to your house."

"Well, it looks like I just saved you a trip. Hop in. I want to take you to my special place where I go when I want to relax and have peace and quiet."

"Well, let's ride. I'm all yours."

"I like the sound of that."

We arrived at Lenora's favorite spot.

"Wow, this is beautiful, Lenora. How did you find this spot?"

"My mom took me here a lot when I was a little girl. We used to camp right over there. So I thought I would save us some money and bring a tent. Help me set it up."

"Awesome, you thought of everything."

We set up the tent, built a fire, and snuggled up with each other against a log, sitting near their campfire. Lenora asked me in a sexy voice, "Baby do you think you could fall in love with a girl like me?"

"You had to ask me that? I've been in love with you since the sixth grade."

We started to kiss passionately. "I think we better take this inside the tent."

After a night of passionate lovemaking, I woke up feeling exhilarated, wearing my heart on my sleeve. I turned and looked at Lenora and saw a very disturbing sight. Her head had been caved in with a huge rock that was laying next to her. I screamed in panic, fearing that I'd done the unthinkable to my first real love. I scrambled out of the tent, saying repeatedly, "What have I done? What have I done? Oh, god, it can't be, not her, not Lenora. (*We warned you, and you challenged us. You made us do it, so pull yourself together. We have to get out of here!* "Oh my god!" *Get up, you fool. It's daylight already. We have to leave quickly!* "Why did you kill her?" *We didn't kill her. You did! Remember Mr. I'm In Control Now? We told you not to cross us. We told you!*)

Suddenly I sat up, screaming loudly, "No!" I was then touched by a soft, warm hand.

"It's okay, baby. You just had a nightmare. It's okay." She grabs me and hugged me tight, reassuring me everything was going to be okay.

"I'm ... I'm sorry, Lenora. I didn't mean to give you such a scare."

"I'm fine. It's you I'm worried about."

"I'll be okay. I guess I just haven't been sleeping much lately with all that's been going on. I'm a little stressed, that's all."

"As long as that's all."

"It is. Come back over here. I'm not done with you yet."

"I like the sound of that."

Morning approached quickly, and the sun shined its light on our faces as we turned and faced each other, gazing into each other's eyes. "Good morning, beautiful."

"Good morning, Mr. Bowers."

"You know what, I think I'll go for a morning swim. Care to join me?"

"I wouldn't miss it, you handsome devil you."

"Oh, come on now. You're only saying that because it's true, Ms. Bingham."

"Oh, you are so bad, Sean Bowers."

"Last one in is a rotten egg!"

"You're on!"

"Hey, wait, aren't you going to put on your bikini?"

"Do you really want me to cover all this up?" She ran and dived in the lake, leaving me standing on the bank. "The water's great, Sean. What are you waiting for?"

I raced toward the lake and dived in. After our swim, we packed up our tent and left, heading back to town. While listening to the radio, we heard the news. It was saying that there had been another murder in Fairfield. I was shocked to hear that, knowing that it wasn't me. I looked to Lenora and said, "Can you believe that? That's so scary."

"Yes, it is, but I'm not afraid as long as I'm with you. I know you'll protect me."

At the police station, Detective Maxwell was pondering what to do with the Bowers kid now that there had been another murder identical to all the others, meaning that he couldn't be their suspect. They arrived at the hospital.

"Detectives, I see you wasted no time in getting here to take me back to your house of horrors you call jail."

"Stow it, kid. We're here to tell you the prosecutor's dropping all pending charges against you."

"Does that mean—"

"Yeah, kid, you're free as a bird."

"So what changed his mind about charging me, Mims?"

"We've had another murder and a missing person to hit our desk in the last twenty-four hours."

"Thank you for coming down and telling me face-to-face."

"Sorry we put you through this, Ronnie. We were just following what leads we had."

"Hey, Dad."

"Hello, son, I see you're in a good mood this morning. What was Mims doing here?"

"He just told me all the charges against me have been dropped." They embraced.

"That's wonderful news."

At the station house, a discussion was taking place between Max and Mims. "I tell you, Mims, that was too perfect."

"What was too perfect?"

"The way this all came to be. I mean, think. Just when we're about to make our charges stick, we have a turn of events that change our outcome. It seems too convenient. We're being played, and I know it."

"Come on, buddy, we're going to find the son of a bitch that's behind these murders, and when we do we're going to nail his ass to the walls of Fairfield jail."

"Mims, I went on a mission last night and decided to go into my father's old files about the Fairfield stalker."

"Well, did you come up with anything?"

"Not much, but I did bring them in so you can help me search for clues."

"What the fuck are you doing? We have enough on our plate. We don't need to be looking through some thirty-year-old cold case files that your daddy had buried in his basement! How is that going to help us?"

"Just trust me. There's something here in these files that's going to shed light on our cases. Think about it, man. All these new cases are very similar to the ones from thirty years ago. It's like we are dealing with the same guy my father was after."

"Hey, take a look at this. It's an old newspaper clipping about a witness to one of the murders. I think your dad was onto something."

"Why do you say that?"

"Because of who the witness is, young William Bowers."

"No shit. Let me see that."

"According to this, young William claimed to have seen a man running away from the scene of the crime. The local news outlets got wind of it when your father's old partner mentioned his name during a news briefing. There's something else. These files don't match up to what my father and his partner typed up at the station on the cases."

"Yeah, but it also says that his old man was really upset about the way the reporters swooped in to question his son."

"Hey, it says here that your father didn't believe young William's story. He believed he wasn't telling the truth about what he had seen. Oh, wow, man, listen to this last passage. 'The Bowers boy seemed more like he was lying, as if he had to protect someone. I truly believe young William Bowers didn't see someone in dark clothing running away from the scene but was in fact the one running from the scene. I let him know I was onto him, but he gave me such a stare that ran chills down my spine. I tell you this young man William Bowers scares me to the bone.' Maxwell, it's dated the day before your father was murdered. You were right. Your father was onto something, and it got him killed."

Back at the abandoned gas station near the motel, I arrived with food and water. I was careful not to be seen by anyone as I ducked under the fence to go inside where Stanley was still tied up. "Stanley, wake up. I have a surprise for you." I took out a five-foot chain with two locks, and I proceeded to put the chain around Stanley's ankle. I locked it in with one of the locks I brought with me. I threw the chain around the center pole in the old building and locked it in. Then I took off the duct tape around Stanley's mouth.

"Please, Sean, I need water."

"It's okay, Stan ole boy, I got you plenty water." I then untied Stanley's hands so he could drink his water. "You can untie your legs. I don't think you will be going anywhere—I mean, being chained up and all."

"Is that food in that bag?"

"Oops, I'm sorry. Here you go. I hope you like pastrami."

"This is fine. Thank you. Can I ask you something, Sean?"

"Sure, we're friends. Ask away."

"Why haven't you killed me yet?"

"Hey, what's your hurry? I mean you're a little determined, aren't you, buddy? Really, if you like I could use this really cool knife I stole from my dad's room yesterday. I don't know, maybe slit your throat."

"Wait a minute, let me see that."

"What, this? I don't think so, Stanley ole boy. Do I look stupid?"

"No, really, I need to see it. Are there markings on it? Look on the hilt. This is very important."

"Wow, you're serious, huh?"

"Sean, please look and see if there are any markings on it."

"All right, all right! Man, what, you've seen this knife before or something? It has markings right here. What do they mean?"

"Where did you get it?"

"I told you I took it from my dad's room yesterday. Stop it now. Just stop it. You're starting to make me nervous. I'm trying to stay in control, and you keep asking me questions like you're in control here. You just stop it. You stop it right now!"

"Okay. It's okay, Sean. Let's just talk. I haven't talked to anyone for days now. I'm a little excited, okay? Let's just talk."

"What do you know about this knife? You've seen it before, haven't you?"

"Yes, but never separated."

"Separated? I don't follow."

"When you found it, was it sealed in a metal box with a circle and a pentagram?"

"No, it wasn't. Why?"

"It's what I was afraid of. Sean, it's the reason you're hearing the voices. Someone broke the seal and opened the box."

(*Why are you wasting our time, you imbecile? You shouldn't be listening to the fat man ramble on! What is he telling you? Why can't we hear your thoughts? What have you done?* "You can't hear my thoughts. Well, that's a new phase in our relationship. You motherfuckers can't hear me! For the first time in my life you can't hear what I'm thinking.")

I started to laugh loudly and almost hysterically.

"Sean! Sean! Listen to me. Can you hear me, Sean?"

"What? Yeah, I hear you, Stanley."

"I know why they can't hear you. Keep the knife on you. Keep it on your person all the time. It's the key."

"The key to what?"

"You're going to have to find the box with the pentagram. I can help you expel them if you find it. That's what you want, isn't it? To stop the voices?"

Back at home William was helping Ronald into the house and looked up to see Detective Maxwell and Mims sitting in their car across from their house. He approached them, shouting profanities. "What the hell do you want now? What, it isn't enough that you almost let my son die in your jail? You have no more reason to harass my family!" William turned around and headed back into his house, but before closing the door he turned and smiled at Maxwell in a very suspicious manner.

"Did you see that, Mims? He's taunting us, daring us to make a play on him."

"So now that you mentioned it, what is our play?"

"We keep digging into his past until we find what my father knew, and then we strike hard and fast."

"Then I guess we better get to work."

The detectives pulled away from the curb, almost hitting another vehicle, when they noticed in the rearview mirror a figure standing in the shadows of an alleyway.

"What do you make of that, Max? The person standing near the alley?"

"I don't know. Let's circle around the block and come up behind him. Stop here. We don't want to spook him. Walk around to the left in case he bolts. You're the youngest. You can be the one to run him down if he does."

"Yeah, thanks. Make *me* chase the guy. Excuse me, sir?"

The man turned around and started walking toward them. "Hey, Officers. Why were you so interested in the Bowers? Wait a minute, don't I know you?" Maxwell asked.

"Hi, Maxie, how have you been?"

"Raymond ... Walter Raymond, is that you?"

"The one and only."

"Hey, Max, you know this guy?"

"Do I? Well, he's only the second best cop to ever walk the streets of East Fairfield. And my father's old partner. So what are you doing back here, Ray, visiting your family?"

"No, we moved away from here twenty-five years ago."

"Then what brings you back?"

"Is it true, Maxie? Is he back and killing again?"

"I can't say. It's an open file."

"Come on, you know me. You know your father and I nearly nailed that bastard thirty years ago."

"He's changed his pattern quite a bit. He seems a lot angrier. Do you have something that you can give us that we're missing, Ray?"

"You bet your sweet ass I do. Take this and nail that bastard to the wall."

"What's this?"

"Everything you need to know."

And just like that, Walter Raymond walked away into the dark alleyway.

"Well, I think we should go home and get some rest so we can have fresh eyes."

"I totally agree. Let's get out of here."

Stanley promised me that he would help me through this, but it was getting late and I was prepared to leave and go home.

"Wait, Sean, you need to know this. What you hold in your hand is only a small piece to the puzzle. We must find that box. It's imperative that you do."

"I'm going to go home now, but I'll be back first light. Here's a blanket and a pillow for you. It's going to get cold out tonight."

"Hey, aren't you worried I'm going to scream for help when you leave?"

"No, I'm actually hoping you're serious about helping me, and if you're here when I get back tomorrow, I'll know. And if you are, then all is forgiven and you can keep the money."

"Just remember, keep it on you at all times, even when you go to sleep."

I left, looking around to make sure I was not seen, and headed home. When I got there, I entered my room, found the duct tape, taped the dagger to my arm, and then lay down and went to sleep. The next morning I got up feeling refreshed and went to my dad's room, but when I got ready to knock I was met by Shelly.

"Let him sleep."

"What?"

"Let him sleep. This is the first time in three weeks he's had a good night's sleep. We should let him sleep as long as he wants too today."

"You know what, you're right. I'll just wait until he's awake."

"Well, I'm headed out. Got a lot to do today. I'll see you later."

"Bye, sis."

I knocked on Leann's door, but she had already left too. Ronald started on his way upstairs, and to my surprise our eyes met, and we immediately hugged.

"Bro, how—"

"Well, apparently when the other murder occurred they realized I wasn't their man and released me."

"Hey, Ronnie, is Dad okay?"

"Of course he is. He's been gone since about six this morning."

"You mean he's not here?"

"No, he told me he had to go see some friends upstate and he'd be back late tonight."

"Oh, really?"

"Well, I guess I better be getting ready to leave myself. I've got a busy day ahead too."

"I think we all do. I'm out."

"Yeah, me too."

I worried that when I arrived at the old gas station I would find that Stanley had escaped. But when I entered, Stanley was still there but he was not chained up.

"Why didn't you just take the money and run, Stan?"

"Didn't I tell you I wanted to help you, son?"

"My father left early this morning."

"Where did he go?"

"He went upstate, something about seeing some friends."

"Did you find the box?"

"I never had a chance to look. My siblings were home, but they all left."

"Let's go then."

"Where to?"

"Your house."

We left the gas station and headed for Stanley's car, still parked in the hotel parking lot. When we arrived at the house, we went inside.

Stanley seemed hesitant for a minute. I looked at him and asked if he was okay.

"Yeah, I'm okay."

"Good. We can start looking in Dad's room. That's the only place in the house none of the kids were allowed."

"Oh my god, what have he and Eleanor been doing?"

"Yeah, it weirded me out too when I first entered his room two days ago. What do you make of this shit?"

"They're ritualistic symbols and relics."

"What are they used for?"

"Sealing away demon spirits. Let's look for that box. It's important that we find it right away."

"Man, I don't even know what I'm doing here, let alone what I'm looking for!"

"Wait, I think I found it."

"What's in it?"

"If I'm correct, nothing."

"We did all this searching for a box full of nothing?"

"Oh, no, we did it so we can return them to where they came from. Let's go!"

"Where?"

"We have to leave, and we have to get far away from this dwelling."

"Okay, you're starting to freak me out now."

"Do you trust me, kid?"

"I don't know. Should I?"

"Let's just go. I'll explain it to you later."

William finally arrived at his destination upstate. It was an old monastery where his father took him thirty years ago to cure him from what was known now as the voices. He pulled in and got out of his car. He looked in amazement as he stood and stared at a very old man staring back at him. The old man approached him and spoke in a scruffy voice.

"Who let them out, William? Who let that abomination out into this world again?"

"Father Kelsey, I can't answer that."

"So you admit they are free once again?"

"Yes, but I'm not sure why or how long they have been exposed to my family."

The father asked, "Which one have they chosen? Which of your family members have they taken into their fold?"

"It's my youngest son, Sean. Father, can we put them back where they belong? Can we stop them again and keep them from tormenting my son?"

"Yes, but first we must find out how they were released. Who is to blame for this travesty? Do you have it, William?"

"I'm afraid not. It's also missing."

"Without the dagger we are powerless. You must find it and bring it and the boy before me. Now hurry. We don't have much time."

"I don't understand. When has there ever been a need to hurry this matter?"

"I'm afraid that your father didn't tell you the story of the voices and how they came to be. You see, long ago, your father lived in Louisiana, deep in the bayou. That's where your family originated. There was a family that practiced black magic that was unheard of at that time. They knew no limits to what they were pursuing. It was dangerous, and that family didn't care. Well, they had a daughter. She was the family's pride and joy. They kept her away from others, because to them she had a special gift. She could talk to the occupant of the underworld, something that was a rare occurrence for her family. They believed that she was the key to their family heritage, one of profit and power. But she wandered off one afternoon and ran upon a young, vibrant boy around her age. They fell in love. That young man was your father. After sneaking around to see each other for nearly three months, she found that she was pregnant. Your father thought the only thing that he could do was ask her father for her hand in marriage. Her family would not accept. They looked upon him with disgrace and asked him to leave and go far away from there, because if he didn't there would be hell to pay. Your father was a stubborn soul, so he went to his love and asked her to leave with him and go far away so that they would never find them. But she was pregnant with child, so they had to wait for the right time. Several more weeks passed, and your father thought enough time had passed. So he took his boat left to him by his father and loaded it with food and water. Then he went and collected his love from near her home. They got in his boat and started to leave, when an old woman known only as the family matriarch raised her hands against them from the shoreline and used her black magic to pull the boat back to shore. He feared for his life after hearing hunting dogs and the voices of her family members approaching. Your father begged the old woman to let them go. He told her he would do the honorable thing and marry her proper when they were far away from the bayou. But the old woman would not release his boat. Instead she cursed your father for all time. She gave him the curse of the wandering souls. The souls of the lost ones were the ones who were trapped between the world of the living and the tormented souls in hell. She wanted him to hear their voices, screaming in torture forever, and if ever he had children, the curse would carry over to them. But she did not know that the young woman your father was trying to take away was with child. That woman's name was Mary Beth, your mother, William. Because of that, the curse passed your father and went into his unborn child. Your father was captured by her family and allowed to live only because the old woman thought her curse was set to run its course. But to the old woman's surprise, your father told her that he would never stop until he and Mary Beth were safely out of Louisiana. And she raised her hand against him once again, but this time your father grabbed her by her arm and said this to her. 'She's having my seed, and nothing you can do to me will stop me short of death.' The rest of the family members of Mary Beth heard what he said and asked her if she was with child. She replied yes. Your father then took from the old woman's side what appeared to be a dagger and grabbed her from behind with the dagger to her throat. He said to her, 'Release me from your curse, old woman, or you will surely die on these shores this day.' She told him, 'I did not know she was with child. The curse is no longer upon you. Take her and leave this place, never to return. The dagger you hold in your hand—keep it for all time.' Then she grabbed his hand and pushed the dagger into her throat. Her black blood ran down the blade. He pulled it out, and her last words were 'With my blood I release you from the voices of torment.' She died right there on those shores. Mary Beth's family moved aside and let your father pass. But they gave him a stern warning that if ever he returned to that place, he would surely die. He took your mother and got in his boat and left, never to return. But he did not know that, as long as the dagger was kept in his presence, the voices would stay in its realm. When he came here, he gave the dagger to me and told me the story of his exploits. I held it for him until it was needed. Months later you were born. Your mother, Mary Beth, did not survive your birthing. Your father moved you to Fairfield, and there he stayed, watching over you, waiting to see if the curse would stay at bay. And then it started, the day he never wanted to face. On your tenth birthday, he noticed you were becoming withdrawn. He used to listen to you late at night, talking as if you were arguing with someone. Then he realized there could be something to the curse. What he didn't want to believe is that it was tormenting his only son. Instead of coming to me, he tried to help you control it. For years he didn't want to believe a family curse would take a toll on his only remaining family member. And then one day out of the blue a woman drove up in front of the monastery. In her hands she held a box with a pentagram carved into its wooden finish. She said to me, 'I'm here because it's going to start.' I asked her what she was talking about. She responded by saying, 'This box is the only thing that would hold them and return them to their realm.' 'Hold who?' I asked. She said, 'The one who will ask him to kill for them.' 'What shall I do with it?' I asked. She told me to dip the dagger in holy water and wipe her blood on his forehead and it will send them in the box. And whatever you do, never open it again or the fury of the Henna curse will once again be released.

She went on to say, she designed the box after the souls had been returned, only to be opened by a descendent of the Henna family. Beware, Father, of those who seek revenge against his bloodline! He has not been forgiven for taking her away. Then the woman walked away, never to be seen again."

"Father Kelsey, did you say the family name was Henna?"

"Yes, of course, William. The old woman whose life was taken while holding onto your father's hand was Mae Henna. She was the leader of the black art in the bayou. Some said she was over 150 years old. Others have said she killed herself so she could become the voice that would torment your father."

"Father Kelsey, my wife's maiden name was Henna. That can't be a coincidence."

Detectives Mims and Maxwell were pondering the files given to them by Walter Raymond. "Hey, Mims, look at this. Ray and my dad were putting the pieces together when suddenly my father was murdered. It says here that the only odd thing about their case was that when old man Bowers sent young Williams away, the murders stopped."

"Wow, that was the key. Maybe they knew all along who their murderer was but they just didn't have enough to arrest him. Why didn't Walter Raymond keep going with this information?"

"I don't know, but I'm sure he had his reasons."

"Why don't we go ask him? He's over at the motel."

They left the station and headed for the motel. Upon arrival they were stopped by Josh, who worked in the motel lobby.

"Detective Maxwell, can I talk to you for a minute?"

"Yeah, what's up—Josh, is it?"

"Yes, sir. I just wanted to know where you are on your investigation."

"You know I can't share that information with you, kid."

"Yeah, but I may have something you need to go forward on your case."

"Well, I don't have all day, kid. Spit it out."

"That Bowers kid—he's been back and forth over at that old gas station for about a week, and then suddenly yesterday he emerges with the fat guy who's been missing on the news."

"Come on, kid. What, you take me for a fool? Ronald Bowers has been locked up for the past two weeks, and then he's been in the hospital, healing from a suicide attempt."

"Ronald? I'm not talking about that Bowers kid. I'm talking about the other one—what's his name, Sean."

"Wait, is that the Bowers kid that signed Murdock's departure sheet?"

"Yeah, only he signed it R. Bowers. You see, that's when I knew."

"That's when you knew what?"

"It's when I knew he was the one committing the murders."

"Okay, slow down. Let's not get ahead of ourselves. Why do you think this kid is our guy?"

"Come on, Detective. He's always been the weird one. The other Bowers kid is the neighborhood fag. He doesn't have the balls to hurt a fly. But that other one, Sean, he's not all there. That guy spends his time talking to himself pretty much all day. He was that way in high school too. That dude was strange. Man, he scared me. If you ask me, he's your guy. He's weird enough to be a serial killer."

"Okay, Maxwell, that just put a different spin on things."

"You're right. I think we need to reinterview Brickshaw's neighbor."

"Thanks, kid, you've been a big help."

"Hey, Detective Maxwell, there wouldn't happen to be a reward for this, would there?"

"I'll tell you what, Josh, if there is, you will be the first to know. What an asshole."

"Yeah, but he gave us some good info, don't you think, Max?"

"I think we should check out that gas station, see if there's something to what that kid said."

"Aw, man, does it stink in here. Smells like piss and shit."

"Damn, Mims, you should be used to it then."

"What the fuck is that supposed to mean?"

"It smells just like your apartment."

"Ha-ha, aren't we the comedian today."

"Is it me or is that a chain wrapped around that pole?"

"Yes, it looks like our friend had a guest staying here for a while."

"Yeah, but it doesn't look like he was here by choice."

"But what are we missing? Josh said that the kid Sean left with Murdock, the missing guy, but they seem to be working together, not forced. If this kid is our killer, maybe he has an accomplice."

"Let's go see Brickshaw's neighbor."

They arrived at Solomon Brickshaw's neighbor's house, and the man walked out on his porch.

"Good day, sir. I don't k now if you remember us, but—"

"I remember you, Detectives. What can I do for you?"

"We'd like to ask you a few more questions."

"Let's have it. I'll help you any way I can."

"When you said you saw the Bowers kid, you meant Ronnie Bowers, right?"

"Oh, for heaven's sake, no. I was talking about the one who delivered the papers, Sean. He's the one who went in the house with Brickshaw. Hell, when the other Bowers kid got here, Brickshaw never opened the door. I'm guessing he was already dead by then, because that's when you guys came and found his body."

"Thank you, sir. We appreciate your help."

"Not a problem. You know, Detective Maxwell, I knew your father. He was a good man and a good friend. He didn't deserve to die like that."

"Thank you, sir. Well, Mims, we just found our killers."

"What do you mean 'killers'? You think he has an accomplice then?"

"Nope. I'm talking about our murderer from thirty years ago and our new murderer today. Like father, like son. All this time it's been right here under our noses and we just didn't see it."

"I don't know. I think we didn't see it because they've had a lot of practice."

"Yeah, but now it's time to pay the piper. It's time we go and make some arrests."

Meanwhile, Stanley attempted to call William on his cell phone. "Hello?"

"William, it's me, Stan."

"What—where the hell have you been?"

"Look, it's a long story. Where are you?"

"I'm upstate. I just left the monastery. I had to talk to Father Kelsey."

"Look, William, I know about everything. Sean's with me. We have to get him to the priest."

"Head this way, Stan. I'll turn around and wait for your arrival."

(*Sean, we need to hear you talk to us. Why won't you talk to the only friends you have?* "No, you're not real. You're not real!")

"Listen to me, Sean. Fight them. Don't let them win!"

"They're screaming so loud, Stan!"

(*You fool, you think we don't know what's going on. Stop it, Sean. You can't win. You must stop this now or we will be forced to hurt you!*)

"Just hold on, Sean. We will be there soon."

(*Sean! Do you have it? Do you have the dagger? We know you can hear us. Take the dagger and stab him with it, and we will no longer need you to do our bidding.*)

I started to rip the tape from my arm that held the dagger.

"What are you doing, Sean? You can't let them win. They are lying to you. They've been lying to you all along."

"I can't help myself. Pull over. They are too strong. Help me, Stan! Help me!"

Stanley pulled over to the side of the road, and I took the dagger and tried to stab him in his chest. Stanley grabbed me by the arm and took the dagger away from me.

"Sean, pull yourself together. We are almost there, and this will all be over soon."

"Okay. I'm okay. Drive."

"Just then a police cruiser pulled up behind us.

"Shit, we don't need this. Lean back, Sean. I need to go in the glove box. Open it up?" Stanley took out a gun and placed it between his legs, out of sight of the officer approaching the vehicle.

"Sir, I noticed you pulled over on the side. Is everything okay?"

"Ah, sure, Officer. We just had an argument, and my son and I were just apologizing to each other. We were just about to pull off when you pulled up."

"Is that right, kid?"

"Yes, sir, Officer."

"Okay, then, you guys be careful and have a good evening."

"Thank you, Officer."

Stanley pulled off, and I kept staring at his gun. "Stanley, I just want to say if I can't control this, you have to kill me."

"Shut the fuck up, kid. Nobody's killing anybody. There's been enough of that going around."

The police officer who pulled them over listened to his radio and heard the APB broadcasting about a blue Buick Riviera that he just pulled over. He called it in, telling dispatch he just pulled over that vehicle and let them go. Suddenly over the radio, Detective Maxwell asked what direction they were headed. He told him the direction and asked who was in the car. The officer told him an older gentleman about fifty-something and a young man between the ages of eighteen and twenty.

"Okay, Officer, this is what I want you to do. Stay back. Don't follow them too close. I don't want you to spook them. These guys are dangerous. Just stay on them, and keep me posted on their whereabouts. We're on our way in your direction."

"Yes, sir, Detective. I'm on it."

William arrived back at the monastery and rushed inside. "Father Kelsey, he's on his way here. He should be here within the hour." William settled down and went into deep thought, trying to put the pieces together about his wife Eleanor. He did not know why Eleanor opened the box to release the entities inside. When he turned around, his focus was on an image walking toward him in the dark hallway of the monastery. Then she stepped into the light and entered the room where he stood.

Father Kelsey stepped out from behind her and said to William, "You need to listen to her."

She looked upon William and said to him, "You are the one who inherited the Henna curse. Years ago you met a young woman who allowed you to sweep her off her feet. The two of you wed and had many children. But then there was the day she went to visit her relatives in Louisiana, not knowing that she would meet the one who would tell her the story of your family, your father. She became distraught and questioned their every word until finally they convinced her that she needed to remember her heritage. And she did so willingly. They told her of the curse and let her know about the dreams she had been having that were keeping her awake at night. The elders warned her of the danger she was in and asked her to go back and find the box with the dagger and bring it back to the family from which it came. But she was being deceived. The elders knew once she touched the box the seal would be broken and the voices would again be free to create havoc. She refused to help them, because she truly loved you, William. She left and returned to Fairfield, several weeks later, when she found out she was again with child. Her dreams were getting worse. She had many more sleepless nights. One of those nights she wandered into your closet and came upon an old chest sitting in the back of the closet. She opened it and heard whispers coming from deep inside the chest. Startled, she dug deeper in the chest to find what it was she was hearing. And there she came upon the box. The whispers grew stronger, and then she did the only thing that would release the voices. She picked up the box, and immediately the seal was broken. She opened it, and the dark forces sealed inside overwhelmed her, knocking her back to the floor. And that's when they entered her body and attached themselves to her unborn child."

"How could you know this? Who are you, and how do you tie in to all this?" William asked.

"I am the one sent to retrieve what belongs to the one I serve. I am here to help you succeed in placing the one back in the box."

Detectives Maxwell and Mims finally arrived at the location the officer called in to them, which was about a half mile outside the monastery. They started to organize and plan how they were going to take down William and Sean with the local authorities.

Stanley and I arrived at the monastery. I was still fighting to keep the voices at bay when we arrived. We rushed inside so that the priest could perform the ritual. They lay me down on a table in front of the altar, and Father Kelsey began. He dipped the dagger in the holy water and took the reconstituted blood and made a sign of the cross on my forehead. The table began to shake violently. Father Kelsey placed the dagger in the box. The voices screaming loudly now could be heard by all in their presence. I began to shake and convulse. The voices were screaming my name. (*Sean, don't let them! Sean, they must fail! Stop it. You can't make us go away. We will always be with you!*) And the entities were thrust into the box, and the lid closed and sealed itself. Suddenly there was calm in the room. The voices were gone, back in the box where they belonged.

"Sean, can you hear me?" asked William.

"Yeah, Dad, it's me. I'm okay. What happened?"

"I'll tell you all about it, son, just not now. Let's get you home and get you some rest."

Father Kelsey took the box and handed it over to the mysterious woman, who hurried down the hallway and out the door.

"Is that it? Is it over for good, Father Kelsey?"

"There's no way of telling, William. All we can do is pray."

"Thank you again, Father, for your help."

Stanley looked at William and began to explain himself, when William told him, "Forget about it. You helped save my son's life. Whatever you did, it's forgiven. Let's go home."

They turned and walked down the dark hallway. When they opened the door, they were met by Detective Maxwell, smiling from ear to ear, as though he had hit the jackpot at a Las Vegas casino. "William Bowers, Sean Bowers, you are under arrest!"

At that moment Stan stepped in front of William and pointed his gun at Detective Maxwell. He opened fire, hitting Maxwell in the chest. The other officers opened fire on Stanley. Bullets flew everywhere. Father Kelsey grabbed me and pulled me down to the floor. The bullets from the officers' guns just missed me and Father Kelsey. But they struck William several times, killing him instantly. Stan too fell dead.

The gunfire stopped, and when the smoke cleared, William and Stanley lay dead on the ground. Detective Mims was yelling, "Hold your fire! Hold your fire!" Detective Maxwell—alive but seriously injured— had survived the onslaught. The officers raced forward, taking me into custody. Mims attended to Maxwell. "Hold on, Max. An ambulance is en route. Where's that ambulance!"

Just then Maxwell looked up at Mims and said to him, "How come you never hold me like this at the office?"

"Maxwell, did I ever tell you you're an asshole?"

"All the time, buddy. All the time."

I was screaming at the officers, "You killed him! You motherfuckers killed him!"

Father Kelsey tried to comfort me as the officers tried to put me in their cruiser. And then I broke down in tears, yelling for my dad. "Dad! I'm sorry, Dad!"

Detective Mims let the EMTs work on his partner and walked over to read me my rights. "Sean Bowers, I'm placing you under arrest for murder. You have the right to remain silent."

I yelled out, "Fuck you! I am remaining silent. I'm happy to be able to hear my own thoughts for a change. Of course you wouldn't know anything about that now, would you, Detective Mims? But I bet your partner knows. They told me all about him and his father."

"Kid, you need to shut your mouth and shut it now!"

"Or what, you're going to hurt me the way you used to beat your ex-wife? Yeah, I know all about your exploits. They told me everything about you, Mims, and your partner too."

"Who the fuck are they, you piece of shit?"

"The voices, the real killer. You have no idea what you're dealing with, Mims. No idea. They will return, and when they do you and your partner will be first on their list."

"Get him out of here before I forget I'm a police officer!"

After leaving the monastery, Mims went back to Fairfield. He first stopped at Fairfield General to check on his partner. "Whoa, you look like shit, man."

"What did you expect when I just had a bullet removed from deep inside my chest cavity?"

"Oh my, you mean you didn't get shot in the face? Damn! How are you, buddy?"

"I've had better days, for sure."

"Did they say when you can get out of here?"

"Maybe a week."

"Great. We have a lot of work to do, so heal fast and get your ass back to work."

"Hey, Mims?"

"Yeah, man."

"Thanks for saving my ass back there."

"You would have done the same for me."

"The kid?"

"He's safely tucked away in a cell, awaiting his court date."

"But he was talking some weird shit when he was arrested. He knew shit about my past that I've never shared with anyone, and he said he knows all about you too. He was rambling on about something having to do with some voices."

"That's just the ramblings of a sick mind. The kid's a serial killer. He'll say anything to save his ass now. What's important now is we solved this case and solved the case of the Fairfield stalker, so let's just relish that for a moment."

"I was now in jail and not allowed visits from my siblings.

"Officer, you must let us see our brother," Leann pleaded.

"Sorry, ma'am, strict orders from top brass. No one in, no one out, until he's been arraigned. You might want to talk to the detective in charge."

"Well, at least tell me if you have news of my father."

"Listen, if I had anything I could help ease your mind with, I'd give it to you, I swear."

"Leann, let's wait for the detective to get here so we can get some answers."

Shelly replied, "Yeah, let's do that."

A television in the background had suddenly been turned up by other officers in the building, unaware that Leann and the rest of Sean's siblings were in the room next to them. "Late-breaking news. There's been a shoot-out in Oldenburg, about two hours outside of Fairfield, with two casualties who have now been identified as Stanley Murdock and William Bowers. Both men were pronounced dead at the scene. One officer was also injured but is expected to recover. Officers say the shootings took place at the old monastery on Bealman Road. It is also said that detectives at the scene went to make arrest two suspected murderers when one of the men pulled a gun and fired a shot, wounding one of the detectives. Officers returned fire. One arrest was made—a young man named Sean Bowers, who detectives say murdered five people, including his own mother Eleanor Henna Bowers. The remaining suspect, Sean Bowers, is being held in Fairfield county lockup."

The room erupted with cheers from the officers occupying the room. "Way to go, Maxwell. He fucking got the bastards."

"You guy are fucking idiots," said Candice. "That's my family you're cheering about being destroyed."

Detective Mims entered the room and turned the television off. "Who are the idiots responsible for this? I got a good mind to have your fucking badges."

"We're sorry, Detective. We didn't know they were here."

"Detective Mims? I'm very sorry about that. That was not the way you needed to find out about your father."

"Then it's true they killed him?" Leann asked.

"We didn't go there to kill anyone, but Mr. Murdock fired a shot and hit Detective Maxwell. The local officers returned fire, and your father was hit multiple times. I'm sorry it had to go down that way, ma'am."

"You're sorry? Are you fucking kidding me? You say that as if you stepped on my foot or something! You killed my father, you bastard!"

"Detective Mims, when can we see Sean?" Ronald asked.

"I can maybe get you in to see him for five minutes. I owe you that much."

Mims escorted them back to where I was being held. "Open up seven!"

"Sean!" They all embrace me with a hug. "Sean, look at me and tell me this is a mistake. Tell me none of this is your fault."

I just stared at my family and said to them, "Don't worry about me. I'm free now."

"What are you talking about, Sean?" Shelly asked.

"The voices. We put them back in the box. They can't hurt anyone anymore. Don't you see, guys, I didn't kill anyone. They did. They made me do it."

"I'm sorry, everyone. We have to leave now," said Detective Mims.

"Hang in there, bro. We're here for you."

"Detective, what is my brother talking about?"

"I don't know, Shelly. He's been talking that way since we arrested him. As a matter of fact, I was going to ask you if any of you knew what he's talking about. Leann, can I talk to you alone for a minute?"

Ah, yeah. Ah, Ronnie, get them home and I'll see you guys shortly, okay?"

"You sure?"

"Yeah, I'll be okay. Mims will bring me home, right?"

"Yeah, sure. We can step in here to talk. I wanted to tell you about our case against your brother and unfortunately your deceased father."

"Did they do it? I mean was my father really the Fairfield stalker?"

"I'm afraid so. We have overwhelming evidence about both your father and your brother."

"So what's going to happen to my brother now?"

"Well, that's up to a judge and jury, but I have to tell you it's not looking good for him. His case calls for the death penalty."

"Detective, why were they at a monastery?"

"That's a good question. I have the old priest in my office. Maybe he can give us something. Father Kelsey, thank you for coming in, sir. This is Leann Bowers, Sean's oldest sister. We were hoping you could shine some light on why this ended up in your lap at the monastery."

Father Kelsey then told Mims and Leann the same story he told William and the story of their mother, given to him by the mysterious woman. After an hour or more of hearing the father tell this strange story, Leann stood in disbelief.

"Wow, this is really hard to swallow, Father Kelsey. I mean, you have to look at this from my perspective, and I'm thinking you're nuts."

"I'm only here to tell you what I know, nothing more, nothing less. Good day to you both." Father Kelsey started for the door, turned, and said, "Let this be your warning. These are not the ramblings of a senile old man. Heed them, and beware of the name Henna. This name brings death to your family."

"Okay, that was different," said Mims. "I'm sorry, Leann, I didn't know we were going to get the next episode of 'The Twilight Zone.'"

"Well, it was interesting, to say the least."

"Hey, listen, let me drop you off at home, and I'll stop back to check on your brother before I call it a night."

Mims dropped Leann off at home and, like he said, returned back to check on me. "Hey, kid, you doing okay?"

"Did he ever tell you about his family's dark secret, Mims?" asks Sean.

"How's that? Maxwell, did he ever tell you about his father?"

"Come on, you don't think he became the asshole he is without cause, do you?"

I started to laugh. "Boy, does he have you fooled. You see, Mims, when the voices left my body, they left me with all the memories of their last victims, all of them, including my father. You see, my father didn't kill Maxwell's father, because he was afraid he was getting close to finding out his secret. He killed him so the murders would stop."

"What are you saying, you sick bastard?"

"Oh, maybe his father dressed up his story so it would look like my father was the Fairfield stalker. Maybe Maxwell knew what his father was and saw him being killed but yet said nothing. Here's a twelve-year-old kid looking out the window on that dark eerie night at the face of a man who buries things in his backyard. One particular night, my father William, followed him. That is when he saw what was being buried. The voices only wanted one other soul to come into their realm—the soul of a mass murderer—so they can mimic what he does to his victims. The voices wanted to learn from the best. By the time they got to me, they perfected his skills and picked up where he left off. His father was the only murder my father ever committed, and your partner knew that."

"Wow, kid, you really are sick. Maxwell said you would say anything to save your ass."

"Come on, you read his father's files. Three bodies were never recovered. They knew they were dead because of the blood at the scene of the crimes. Those three were special to him."

"You know what, Sean? I look forward to seeing you get the needle. Good night, freak."

I started to laugh as Mims walked away. The farther away he got, the louder my laughter got. It echoed through the halls of the jail.

It had been six weeks, and the jury found me guilty of all charges and sentenced me to death. Maxwell had been back to work now for five of those six weeks.

"Well, he gets the needle, just like we hoped," Max said.

Mims replied, "Sorry if I don't feel like celebrating."

"Why the long face? You look like you just lost your best friend."

"You know, I've been looking over your father's files every day since that trial started, and I came across a few things that didn't make sense."

"What difference does it make? One murderer's dead, and the other one's headed for the needle. Relax, man."

"So tell me, how much did you know about your father?"

"Where are you going with this?"

"I'm just saying, how did you feel about seeing him bury bodies in the backyard? I mean, you knew— right?—about his secret, the one he was so adamant about blaming William Bowers for?"

"I don't know what you're talking about, and this conversation is over."

"Your father harassed William and his father, because he knew William followed him each night after his shift. Watching him work, killing those innocent people, and to this day you would stand behind that badge and pretend it never happened."

"Who have you been talking to? There's no way you could have obtained that information.

"So it's all true, Benton?"

"You calling me by my first name now?"

"I used to respect you and everything you stood for. Now I don't even know who you are." Mims turned and walked out the door.

"Hey, Mims, that bastard killed my father! He had to pay for what he did, didn't he? Didn't he! What are you going to do, huh? What are you going to do!"

Mims pulled up in front of the Bowers residence and went up to the door. He rang the doorbell, and Leann answered. "Detective Mims, how are you?"

"I'm as well as to be expected."

"What brings you by? Because you don't have to apologize to my family for doing your job."

"No, I'm here on another matter. Are the rest of your siblings home?"

"Yes, let me get them."

When they all gathered, he told them that their father wasn't the Fairfield stalker and he would do everything in his power to clear his name.

"But you see, your father only murdered Officer Maxwell to stop him from killing more people. After that your grandfather took him away to get him some help. And it was the perfect opportunity for his partner, Walter Raymond, to suspect your father as the killer. He never thought it could be Maxwell, because he was a police officer, so he never put the pieces together. I've talked to Mr. Raymond since I obtained this information, and he agrees that, in fact, your father stopped the Fairfield stalker. Well, now you know the whole story. You've been walked through the life of a serial killer."

"So, now, I need you to do the right thing, Mims, by making sure my family is taken care of."

"You know, Sean, I can talk to some friends of mine, and they can still make a case for you and try to get you a stay of execution."

"Nah, I'm just going to let this happen. Man, it's time to give up the fight. It's been three years, and I'm tired. So did you really just walk away from being a detective and being a part of Fairfield history?"

"Yeah, after we found the remains of the stalker's last three victims in Maxwell's backyard, I just didn't want to be a part of that history. The lies and the deceit were too much for me. Besides, your sister stayed on my ass about writing this story, so I wasn't going to have time with the baby coming and all."

"Wow, how big is she now?"

"Oh, my bad. I've got pictures for you to look at. She wanted me to tell you she decided on a name for him."

"Cool, what's it going to be?"

"William Patrick Mims."

"Well, you tell her I approve and you guys make a great couple. I got to tell you, I didn't see that coming. But now I see that you are the right man for her and she loves you, man. You take care of them for me, and don't forget about Stanley Murdock's wife. She deserves some compensation out of this too. Was the money where I said it was?"

"Yep, every cent. Ronald finished school and reopened the family business, and Candice and Shelly work there with him. He's expanding now."

"Oh, yeah? That's great."

"Candice will be graduating this summer, with honors, of course. They took the money and gave

Stanley's wife half and put the rest back into the business. After Leann found Dad's life insurance policy, it pretty much paid for school for Candice. Even Shelly went back to school and got her degree in accounting. I think they're going to be okay, Sean."

"So tell me, what ever happened to Benton Maxwell?"

"Well, after the local newspapers suspiciously got wind of his father's extracurricular activities as the Fairfield stalker, he decided to eat his gun. The poor bastard actually left a suicide note, apologizing to the families of his father's victims."

"Hmm, tough break. I would have thought he would have waited until they pushed the plunger on me."

"You know, your trial was tough on the family, but they made it through. And now they are all leading their separate lives and succeeding in their endeavors because of you in a strange way."

"No, don't give me that credit. If it weren't for you standing up to Maxwell and pushing him to tell the truth about his father, my family would have been looked upon like lepers."

"Haven't heard any more voices, have you?"

"Not ever again after tonight."

"Sean, I didn't mean it like that. I'm sorry."

"No, it's fine. I'm at peace with myself now. I just hope this is the end of it."

"Oh yeah, I almost forgot. Your daughter sent this for you to take to heaven with you, and I swear those are her words."

"So Lenora told her?"

"Only that her daddy has to go to heaven to help God take care of Grandpa and Grandma."

"Wow, it's a tiny teddy bear. Do me a favor?"

"Anything."

"When I'm gone, put this in my casket next to my heart and tell Lenora I said I'm sorry I couldn't be around to see our baby grow up and that I will always love her."

"Sure, I will do that for you."

"Mr. Bowers, it's time. Hey, would you like the priest to walk with you?"

"No, warden, just Mims. He's the only one who makes me feel comfortable."

"Suit yourself. We need to put on the restraints, son."

"Okay, let's get this party started, warden. I have somewhere I have to be."

"You ready, Sean?"

"Yeah, Mims."

The warden yelled, "Dead man walking!" And they started the slow walk to the death chamber.

"Hey, Mims, this is going to be a hell of an ending for your book."

"The funny thing is I'm not done yet."

They arrived at the chamber, strapped me in, and opened the curtains for the witnesses to gaze upon me in my last moments of life. They asked me if I had any last words.

"Hell, yes, I do. Today I die, but you will never kill the voices in my head, for soon I will be them and they will be me. On this night the voices will reemerge and wreak havoc on you all. And this time they will be under my control."

They covered Sean's face and turned the key, releasing the poisons. Sean drifted away into darkness and was pronounced dead.

Two weeks later, Leann and her husband, Allen Mims, were preparing to receive guests for their baby shower. As guests started to arrive, they were both very happy that all their friends were there, bringing gifts and well wishes. There was box after box and bag after bag of so many wonderful items.

"Allen, what are we going to do with so much stuff for our baby?"

"Well, I suggest we put it all to use, sweetheart."

"Yeah, I know, but by the time we get to some of it, he will have outgrown most of it."

They both laughed. Leann stood up and thanked their friends for all the wonderful gifts and offered them refreshments. As Allen was engaged in conversation with the husbands of their friends, Leann smiled and stared at her loving husband. Then she felt the baby kick. He kicked with such force she had to sit down. Allen looked over to see his wife in distress and rushed to her aid.

"You okay, sweetie?"

"I'll be fine. Put your hand here. He's kicking."

"Wow, that's amazing, honey. This kid is strong, just like his father."

"I'll be sure to tell him that."

"Ha-ha, I see you haven't lost your sense of humor."

"Oh my, he's kicking so hard."

"Maybe you should lie down, honey. You've been on your feet for quite a while."

"No, baby, we have guests. I don't want to just leave them to fend for themselves."

"Okay, then sit here and put your feet up. I'll get your sisters to help out."

"Thank you, Allen. You're a godsend."

After the baby shower was over, everyone was very exhausted. Allen told Leann that he had to go out for a while and he'd be gone for about an hour. He went out to the cemetery with Shelly and Candice to put flowers on the graves of their father, William, and brother Sean.

"Wow, it's been four years since Daddy's death, and I still miss him, Shelly."

"I miss him too. I hope Sean found peace."

"I'm sure he's resting peacefully, girls, especially after knowing that all of you were going to be okay. By the way, where's Ronnie? I thought he was going to meet us here."

"I'm right here, guys. You know me, always late. The flowers are beautiful, ladies. I just wish we were able to put flowers on Mom's grave too. I don't understand these Hennas and why they fought us so hard to take Mom's body back to Louisiana. We don't even know them, and then they told us to stay away from Louisiana, like we wanted to visit their weird asses."

"It's funny how we never knew Mom was a Henna. Didn't we go to school with a Henna?"

"Yeah, we did, and all this time he was our cousin."

"Hey, one thing I do remember about him was that he used to kick the shit out of Sean. Man, Sean hated that guy. What was that kid's name?"

"It was Reese. Reese Henna. Sean used to call him the terror of Fairfield. I wonder what ever happened to him and his family, for that matter."

"They are still around. I used to think he had a crush on me because he always stood up for me in school."

"Wow, Shelly, I never knew that."

"Candice, just because Ronnie used to tell you all his business doesn't mean I was going to tell you mine."

They all laughed and started to walk back to their cars. Candice stopped and said, "Hey, guys, maybe we should pay Reese and his family a visit one day. After all, they are related to us on Mom's side."

"I agree. It's about time we met the other side of our family. What do you think, Allen?"

"I think you should stay far away from those people. There's something that just doesn't sit right with me about them. We better head back before Leann gets worried."

"Who would have thought you and the tattoo freak would get married someday?"

"Hey, I love her. What can I say?"

"Hey, I remember when you and Leann used to stare each other down whenever you and Detective Maxwell came to our house. She'd say, 'That Mims guy is so good-looking.'"

Back at the house the doorbell rang, and Leann got up to answer the door.

"Hi, Leann?"

"Hi, do I know you?"

"You might not remember me, but I went to school with you guys. My name is Reese."

"Oh, yeah, I do. You're the terror of Fairfield."

"What?"

"It's a long story. What can I do for you?"

"Well, I'm your cousin."

"How's that?"

"My name is Reese Henna. Your mother and I were related."

"Oh my god, you're pulling my leg."

"Anyway, I heard about the baby shower and brought you a gift from the family. I have to go, so enjoy it."

"Thank you, Reese."

Leann sat the gift on the table and started to open it.

"What's this? What a weird-looking box."

The minute she touched it, she heard voices screaming, and she fell back on the couch, holding her stomach, when a strange entity appeared and entered her stomach. She screamed and fainted.

(*Hello, nephew, I'm your uncle Sean, and we're going to be good friends.*)

Loud laughter ensued, echoing throughout the entire house.

The end.

(*No, let's just say the beginning of the end. Ha ha ha ha ha ha ha ha!*)